★ NIGHT ★
VISION

Karin Kallmaker

Bella
BOOKS
2008

Writing as Karin Kallmaker:

The Kiss that Counted
Christabel   Finders Keepers
Just Like That   Sugar
One Degree of Separation   Maybe Next Time
Substitute for Love   Frosting on the Cake
Unforgettable   Watermark
Making Up for Lost Time   Embrace in Motion
Wild Things   Painted Moon
Car Pool   Paperback Romance
Touchwood   In Every Port

Writing for Bella After Dark:
In Deep Waters 1: Cruising the Seas
18th & Castro
All the Wrong Places
Tall in the Saddle: New Exploits of Western Lesbians
Stake through the Heart: New Exploits of Twilight Lesbians
Bell, Book and Dyke: New Exploits of Magical Lesbians
Once Upon a Dyke: New Exploits of Fairy Tale Lesbians

Writing as Laura Adams:
The Tunnel of Light Trilogy:
Sleight of Hand
Seeds of Fire

Feel free to visit www.kallmaker.com

Visit

Bella Books

at

BellaBooks.com

or call our toll-free number

1-800-729-4992

Bella Books, Inc.
P.O. Box 10543
Tallahassee, FL 32302

First Edition Naiad Press 1997
First Bella Books Edition 2009

This novel was originally released under the pen name Laura Adams in 1997 by Naiad Press.

Printed in the United States of America on acid-free paper.

Editor: Lisa Empson
Cover Design: Linda Callaghan

ISBN: 10: 1-59493-119-4
ISBN: 13: 978-1-59493-119-2

For Katherine Janeway, DeLenn,

Drake and Pyanfar Hani,

women I would follow across the known

and unknown universe

About the Author

Among Karin Kallmaker's more than twenty-five romances and fantasy-science fiction novels are the award-winning *Just Like That, Maybe Next Time, Sugar* and *18ᵗʰ & Castro* along with the bestselling *Substitute for Love* and the perennial classic *Painted Moon*. Two dozen short stories have appeared in anthologies from publishers like Alyson, Bold Strokes, Circlet and Haworth, as well as novellas and dozens more short stories with Bella Books. She began her writing career with the venerable Naiad Press and continues with Bella. Her novels have been translated into Spanish, French, German and Czech.

She and her partner are the mothers of two and live in the San Francisco Bay Area. She is descended from Lady Godiva, a fact which she'll share with anyone who will listen. She likes her Internet fast, her iPod loud and her chocolate real.

All of Karin's work can now be found at Bella Books. Details and background about her novels are at www.kallmaker.com.

Chapter 1

"None of this is going to make any sense." I rested my chin on my hand as I struggled to keep eye contact with the intense woman across the table from me. "You're going to think we're all one step away from strapping on brand-new Nikes and sprinkling cyanide on our applesauce."

Tamar had a way of looking at me—not right in the eyes, but as if she were trying to see right into my brain. She was looking at me that way now. "I'm very good at telling fact from fiction. I'm not going to assume you're looking to catch a ride on the next comet out of the galaxy."

I looked down at the fancy compact digital recorder she had set up on the tiny dinette table. The wind rocked the little motor home, and I glanced around at my companions. Having elected me the one to tell Tamar the whole truth and nothing but the truth, they were grabbing what little sleep they could. The strain of the past two weeks showed on every face.

Vina was snoring delicately and frowning on the little built-in couch. Rose was curled on a sleeping bag in the few feet available along the front of the bathroom and kitchen area, but I doubted she was asleep. I could just see Geri's arm and shoulder in the overhead. JT was propped up in the passenger seat in the cab. Her fingers moved slightly, as if she dreamed.

Dreams—that was where it had all started. The wind snapped around the motor home, and sand spattered against the windows. "Stuck in the Middle with You" played in stereo in my head.

Tamar prompted me with, "Begin at the beginning."

"I'm not one of those people who remembers their dreams," I said. "Every once in a while I remember—like showing up at work in my pajamas. Everyone has that kind of dream. Anxiety, I guess."

Tamar nodded. Her eyes told me to go on.

"Three weeks ago I started having dreams that I remembered..."

I had awakened drenched in sweat for the third night. The Santa Ana winds rattled the window screens. My ears were ringing as I struggled out of my twisted and tangled bedclothes.

The dream had changed. The previous two nights I'd dreamed of falling from a great height. A noisy dream, shaking, sirens blaring. My sinuses were seared with the smell of burned wiring. In an instant the noise stopped. But I was still falling, now toward a blurred chessboard, and I fell and fell and kept falling, not for a few seconds, but for minutes that seemed to stretch out longer the second night. The dream ended with a bone-jarring thud that was followed by an even more terrifying darkness.

Tonight it had been different. I had been panting while I slept and I thought it was strange that I knew what I had been doing while I was dreaming. I'd panted when the dream darkness ended with a brilliant light and searing heat. I had screamed when the dream me had tried to stand, then shrieked as I fell back to the hot earth, my arms itching and burning as if stung by a thousand bees.

Now I knew I was awake, but I could not quite shake the memory of the pain, as if the dream still continued to envelop me.

I rolled over and rustled through the pile of dirty clothes

2

on the floor until I came up with the remote. *Nick at Nite* was showing an old Bob Newhart rerun. Suzanne Pleshette's husky voice saying "Bob" drove away the last of the dream's fog.

I told myself I wasn't afraid to go back to sleep. I tell myself lots of lies. Three nights of broken sleep were taking their toll on my already precarious sense of humor toward life.

"Julia Madison, you look like hell," Carol said. "Honestly, you're going to be single forever unless you make some effort."

I looked at Carol dully, too tired for the show of vanity I knew I should have displayed. "As if I haven't already dated or lived with every single gay woman in this town," I said, without heat. "I refuse to start with the ones already in couples, and straight women are right out. Been there, done that."

Carol was shaking her head at me. "Are you sure it's quits for you and Mari?"

"It's been quits for six months, as you well know. She and Fran seem quite happy."

"Oh, yeah. I forgot about Fran." Carol took a bite out of her sandwich while I picked listlessly at the tuna noodle casserole that had been today's cafeteria treat. I was well aware that lunch for a buck-fifty was beyond cheap and was a huge help to my tight budget. But sometimes the bland fare reminded me too much of my life, my job, and Fresno.

Carol tsked. "I don't know how you eat that stuff." Her sandwich bulged with sprouts and watercress and looked too healthy to be edible. Carol always watched what she ate. She had a figure that would make just about any poet cry, and yet she was always trying to lose five pounds. Her big Amerasian eyes were always filled with good humor and compassion. With all that going for her she was just as single as I was. In the last few months I'd moved on to "why bother" while Carol was still hoping Mr. or Ms. Right was around the corner. She believed in keeping her options open.

"It's cheap and filling. And it helps me make my mortgage

payment since I'm now paying for the house by myself and buying out Ms. Marigold Jane Tempest's share."

"You may not live to see the last payment eating that stuff. It must be loaded with either fat or cornstarch to be thick like that. And those noodles have probably got egg yolk in them—cholesterol."

I speared a pea and held it up. "Vegetable. This is a vegetable." I ate it. "I have now eaten a green vegetable."

"Technically, that's a legume."

I pursed my lips at her. "I'm going to go for a run tonight anyway."

Carol subsided, knowing that on the topic of exercise I had her beat. She ate better than I did, but I ran a 10K whenever the opportunity presented itself and every other year I trained myself up to do the Sacramento Marathon. Thank God this was an off year. A doctor had told me I had a heart like a horse—a compliment I hadn't appreciated when I was 20, but twenty years later I was counting on it. I knew that the king of running, Jim Fixx, had keeled over from a heart attack. It would happen to me if I didn't change my ways, but change was too hard.

I regarded the noodle on the end of my fork with all the enthusiasm I could find, which was none. In spite of being an overgrown small town, Fresno was a relentless force. The raisin capital of the world boasted long, hot summers and searing sunshine. Sooner or later everyone who lived in Fresno ended up a raisin. The moment I'd moved from the Bay Area to Fresno I'd been doomed to petrification. Marigold Jane Tempest had only accelerated the inevitable.

My life had had less cholesterol in it when I'd been living with Mari. But lately cholesterol was my comfort food. It came in such nice forms. Toast with real butter, milk chocolate, whole milk on Wheaties, cinnamon roll pudding, ribs-to-go from Ernie's Rib Hut—Carol only knew the half of it. I never really gained any weight, but I was substituting bad calories for the better calories I knew I should be eating. I felt lousy, and one dream-free night would have made a big difference.

I hadn't told Carol about the dreams because I didn't know what to say. We were close at work, finding camaraderie in our sexual deviance, but at work only. About four months ago I'd realized that all the women Mari and I had called friends were really Mari's friends. I'd gotten the distinct impression from some that Mari's attempts to reform me into an acceptable dyke had failed. I ate too much red meat, had been caught red-handed at a women's camping weekend reading a John Grisham mystery, and I watched way, way too much television. Mari's circle wasn't one that appreciated the ability to name the Brady kids (which was so easy) or sing the theme from *All in the Family*.

Cholesterol filled the gap in my life, but just barely.

So how could I mention the dreams to Carol? And what would I say anyway? I'd never clearly remembered my dreams before, and I don't believe in all that Freudian and Jungian dream analysis stuff anyway. Well, some of it makes sense. A falling dream is probably anxiety. I was probably just stressed. I knew I was stressed. Stress was responsible for everything wrong with my life.

Did I mention that I tell myself lots of lies?

But it was the same dream two nights in a row, and then last night it had changed from a scary dream to a petrifying nightmare that had gotten even worse when I'd looked in the mirror. How could I show Carol the faint red pinpricks all up and down my arms and tell her I got them in a dream?

Carol was packing up her lunch debris, and I realized it was time to go back to work. She accepted my apology for being antisocial with one of her cheery waves. I slouched back to my desk and flipped on my monitor. Another slew of files had been put in my inbox, and now the in stack was higher than the out, a situation I hated.

If I concentrated on my work I would be able to resist the urge to peek at my forearms again. The last time I'd peeked the marks were still there. I told myself the next time I looked they would be gone. But there was no reason to look now. I could look when I got home. Later tonight. And the marks would be gone because I'd only imagined them in the first place.

Trying to find some enthusiasm, I attacked the stack and began making my computer log entries and phone calls. It was one of those days when I took glee at the faint gasp I always heard when I said the words, "This is Julia Madison from the Internal Revenue Service."

When I changed into my running shorts and tank top there were no marks in sight. I had imagined them, just as I had been telling myself all day. I was glad I hadn't said anything to Carol.

It wasn't the best training decision, but I found myself going much farther than my usual four miles. I chose a route that ran into the wind on the final leg just for the extra energy drain. In the back of my mind was the idea that I would exhaust myself and sleep the night through without a dream.

After my run I showered to get the wind-driven dust out of my nose and eyes, then called Domino's. I settled in front of the TV with a pepperoni thick crust and a pint of Chocolate Berry Mint ice cream, a disgusting-sounding concoction with little to redeem itself beyond being delicious and quite, quite comforting. I let *Nick at Night* take me back to the quick and easy denial of the Sixties and Seventies. One twitch of the nose and Samantha Stevens could get a good night's sleep. It wasn't the first time I wished I were her. When I was a teenager I had wanted her powers in the worst way.

When I snapped awake, the *Rhoda* rerun had given way to the infomercial for the Psychic Readers Millenium. One call to their nine hundred number and I would know if a tree was going to fall on my house or if twins were in my future as either romantic interests or offspring. It was three twenty-five in the morning, and I hadn't escaped the dream. My heart was pounding harder than it did during a run.

It took all my nerve to go into the bathroom and look at my

6

arms in the mirror.

The pinpricks were back.

I couldn't sleep after that. I paced around the house, tried to watch more television, but nothing I did could get rid of the memory of my screaming and the nanosecond of excruciating pain when my arms were...bitten or stung.

I tried to tell myself that the cafeteria was putting MSG or something else in the food and that I was having an allergic reaction.

With practice you can know you're lying to yourself and not even care.

It was Friday. I called in sick. I hadn't wanted to give in to sleep during the day because it would throw off my diurnal rhythms. Mari had believed in diurnal rhythms, moon tides, sun signs and harmonic convergences. The last I heard from her, she and Fran were vacationing in Sedona to do the Vortex thing.

Screw you, Marigold Jane Tempest, I thought, not for the first time. After scrambled eggs and toast, I cuddled under my favorite blanket on the sofa at nine A.M. and hoped my sleep would be dream free. I was prepared to flip channels until I found something stupefying enough to put me under.

I fell asleep so fast I didn't even get as far as turning on the TV.

Coughing. My throat was so dry. I stumbled on...crusted sand that hadn't known an ocean for eons. My eyes seemed full of grit, and I could feel the sting of blowing grit on my face. After a while I rested, then continued my stumbling journey toward distant mountains that seemed made of white. Snow? Water? I was so thirsty.

The dream went on without much change. I was hot, dry, and I walked and walked. After a while I realized I was whimpering as much as a completely dry throat would let me. The mountains didn't seem to get any closer, and the sun was relentless. Any skin that wasn't covered with my white jumpsuit was turning red.

7

There was a low rumbling behind me and I turned, blinking against the setting sun in my eyes. A dark presence was silhouetted against the dirty orange sky. It seemed to surge across the surface I was struggling over, and I turned away, somehow finding the strength to run. Panic turned into grim concentration. Two puffs out, inhale fully, and always watch the footing.

The white mountains refused to grow any closer. A glance over my shoulder told me the machine was slowly gaining on me.

I woke up sobbing for breath. I rolled off the sofa, gasping, and then clambered my way to the kitchen where I downed two Snapple pink lemonades in as many minutes. I splashed water into my dry eyes and then took a cool shower to soothe away the memory of sunburn. I inhaled the moist air into my aching sinuses and lungs.

Great, just great. My falling dream was now a chasing dream. My legs trembled as if I really had been running.

I was chased through most of the night, part of Saturday, and well into Sunday. Even when I was awake I could feel the flutter of panic in my heart. I found myself double-checking that the doors were locked. When I went to the market I caught myself looking over my shoulder in the cereal aisle. By Sunday night I had a stunning headache that sent red fire along my optic nerves.

I was exhausted. Marathon exhausted. Even fifteen minutes of motionless relaxation and deep breathing didn't slow my heart rate or respiration. I was gasping for extra air I didn't need. It wasn't long before I was dizzy with extra oxygen and my eyes wouldn't stay open. The moment they closed I was caught again, running again. But the panic had changed. It was almost exuberance—the mountains that had seemed so distant were just a few minutes ahead. They were steep hills covered in white— snow meant water.

The last few steps to the first hillside that surged up out of the sand were painless. Water. With water I could do anything. The figure behind me, getting closer with every dream, was of no consequence. Water was within my reach. I clambered up the hillside, ignored the bite of sharp-edged plants into my fingers. One more pull upward—

I plunged my hand into the white. It wasn't snow. It was dry powder.

I was rolling down the hillside. The disorientation made me sick to my stomach. I almost woke up, but I couldn't quite pull myself out of it.

I blinked sand out of my eyes and looked up at the hostile brown-blue sky. Every muscle ached. My lungs were bursting. I was so weak. I shouldn't have tried...I should have...should have done something. It wasn't clear what I should have done, but my self-recrimination was clear. I examined my powder-covered hand, then in my dream and in my bed, I went limp and plunged into an abyss of despair.

I woke up sobbing inconsolably. All of a sudden I remembered when my mother had thrown away my Mrs. Beasley doll because I hadn't done my chores. I cried for what seemed like hours, for Mrs. Beasley and for bad dreams. My headache escalated from splitting to excruciating.

I hate Valley Fair Hospital's HMO setup, but that's where I ended up Monday morning. The headache was no better for cold compresses, hot showers, Excedrin, Advil, Aleve and a Vicodin left from minor knee surgery last year. I had tunnel vision and couldn't hear anything but the screech of pain in my ears. I ping-ponged between believing it was a food allergy, a thyroid gone haywire and the certainty that I had a terminal brain tumor.

I took a cab to the hospital. I just wanted something to make me sleep so I could go back to work and let the absolutely ordinary drill of the day get my life back on an even keel. Sleep would cure everything.

After waiting for almost two hours, I was interviewed by a nurse practitioner who took my blood pressure and temperature. Talking was difficult. She kept asking me to speak up. Finally she left me in a little room that was at least cool and dark. Another half-hour's wait was rewarded with a doctor whose manner seemed sympathetic.

"How long have you been having these headaches?" The doctor looked down at the notes the nurse had taken, then fixed his clinical gaze on me as I stumbled for an answer.

"Well, I didn't start having them until I started sleeping badly." It was an effort to speak above a whisper. "I haven't had a good night's sleep since Tuesday of last week, and the headaches started yesterday."

"Hmm." He made a note, then did a physical exam that included looking in my ears and listening to my heart. He measured the extent of my tunnel vision, then tried to look in my eyes with that bright light pencil thing. My eyes teared so badly that he gave it up.

Finally, he said, "I'd usually recommend a CAT scan, but I think that I'll first try a simple sleeping medication. It may very well be that if you did get some better quality sleep the headaches would stop. So I'll write you a prescription for sleeping pills, but if they don't help come back right away and we'll do tests."

"Can you give me something for the pain? I took a leftover Vicodin, and it didn't do squat."

He frowned, then said he'd be right back. "Right back" was about fifteen minutes, but he had a packet in his hand. He made a note on my chart as I downed the two pills with some tap water.

"You'll have to take a cab home or have someone pick you up," he said. "I can't let you drive after taking those."

"I came in a cab." He made another note on my chart and left. I dressed slowly, and by the time I left the examining room the pills were having some effect. The ringing in my ears subsided. I had the sudden urge to giggle.

I found my way to the main lobby with only three wrong turns, but I didn't care. I smiled at strangers and gave the pharmacist my best goofy grin. She was serious, but cute, as she explained the prescription to me. One little silver pill would result in four to six hours of sleep, and no driving within six hours of taking a pill—I got it, yes I do, I assured her. What a cutie. My vision had almost returned to normal by the time I got into a cab.

At home I had some Phish Food ice cream and a bologna sandwich. I sang the Oscar Mayer bologna song off and on for most of the afternoon. I had never before noticed how uproariously funny most commercials are.

When the sun went down I toddled off to bed. I said hello to the little silver pill, swallowed it, and then that was that.

Oddly enough, when I woke up in the morning, I had the feeling that I had dreamed, but I didn't remember any of it. My headache was back at a fraction of the previous level, so I decided I would go to work.

I managed to get through the day. My inbox was frightening, but my supervisor, Emily, rightly interpreted my pallor and fatigue as true illness, not the result of a long weekend in Vegas. I felt a little bit hopeful that the dreams were behind me. Medical science had helped me—someday I would tell Marigold Jane Tempest that.

When I was driving home I had the oddest sensation—I felt as if I was blacking out, but I wasn't. I was wide awake and mostly functional. But I kept blinking away the mercurial illusion of the dancing gray rags I've seen the two times I'd fainted in my life—both during marathons. The sensation finally faded away, and I went to bed early, but not before I had some ribs and cole slaw from Ernie's.

One little silver pill and I woke up Wednesday morning feeling like a million bucks. I had slept deeply, but instead of feeling like I just didn't remember dreaming I knew that I hadn't dreamed—at least not one of the new dreams. I'd dreamed whatever I used to dream that I never remembered or even suspected. The bad dreams were gone.

Even Carol noticed the little hop in my step—and that I'd combed my hair and taken the time to accessorize a belt with my pantsuit.

"My god," she said. "It's a human being in that body."

"I'm a new woman," I told her. I believed it.

I didn't know then what I know now. It's not unusual for a tune to get stuck in my head—it happens to everybody. I mean, sing just once, "There was a farmer, had a dog, and Bingo was his name-oh," and see? There you are. You'll be hearing it all day. Hum along with something in the supermarket and you'll be looking up the lyrics online because you can't quite remember them and it's driving you nuts until you know if it's "Jesus was a country boy" or "Cheeses for the monkey boy." It happens to everybody.

I attached no importance to the fact that for most of that Tuesday I heard "The Entertainer." That's the ragtime piano piece by Scott Joplin that was used in *The Sting*. It's not an unpleasant piece of music.

I had been free of headaches and slept well the night before, so, in deference to the extensive conditioning Marigold Jane Tempest had given me about the evils of unnatural remedies dished out by the medical establishment, I decided to skip that night's little silver pill.

I dreamed, but it wasn't very scary. I could hear the ragtime music, and mostly I dreamed about sleeping and dozing and waking a little and then dozing off again. I slept pretty well.

I presented myself to Carol on Wednesday morning. She approved my well-brushed hair—only slightly the worse for the Santa Anas—the necklace and earrings I'd chosen, and generally complimented me on looking like less of a troll.

It wasn't until after lunch that I began to feel uneasy. A little claustrophobic. I wanted to gasp for breath.

This is silly, I told myself, but then I felt my cafeteria lunch turn over in my stomach. I beat it to the ladies' room, just in case. I sat down in a stall and wondered whether I really was going to throw up.

I finally did. I hate throwing up. I've never understood how people with bulemia can do it. Some things are just not natural. Throwing up and any member of the Bush family performing any sort of sexual act are on my list. Ugh.

It's just food poisoning, I thought. Just a little salmonella in the whatever-that-was they served for lunch. I wiped my face with some toilet paper and then, all in a rush, I was overwhelmed with terror.

One moment I was clutching the toilet a little dizzily and the next I had leaped to my feet looking for an escape—a way out, any way out. A scream bubbled in my throat. Part of me knew that in less than forty-five seconds I could be out of the ladies' room and into the elevator on my way to the ground floor. A flash of ID, a quick step through the metal detectors and I'd be in open air.

But most of me was sure I was trapped. I was shaking my arms as if to get something off my wrists. My legs felt as if they were weighted in cement.

I clawed the door open. Motion helped. I knew I could get out. But when I stopped moving the urge to break out of imaginary bonds came back as did the mind-racking terror. I leaned on the counter and looked into my wide-open eyes. My skin was the color of wallpaper paste.

Carol and her cubicle neighbor Annette came in, took one look at me, and stopped in their tracks. I realized I was panting like a rabid animal.

"Jeez, Julia, what's wrong? You look like—"

"I just threw up my lunch, that's all." I sounded almost normal to my own ears, but Carol boggled at me.

"Sit down on the sofa," she said. She put her arm around my shoulder. It became a tentacle, snaking around my neck, choking me. The scream threatened to break out of me again.

I thrust her away. "No, I've got to go home. Must have been that awful food in the cafeteria."

Annette said, "There was probably ptomaine in the soup or something. Have lots of clear liquids." Annette was a mom, and her advice for almost anything was clear liquids.

I sidled toward the door, afraid they would get between me and it. "Tell Emily I had to go, okay?"

"You stay here, Julia. I'll go get your purse for you so you don't have to walk all the way across the floor and back." Annette slipped out quickly.

Carol looked very concerned. "I'll call you later, okay?" I was on the verge of screaming, and I think Carol knew it. "Maybe you should go to the doctor."

I shook my head. I needed my little silver pill and sleep. Annette returned with my purse, and they walked me to the elevator, parting with assurances that I'd feel better in the morning.

I drove too fast, but luckily I didn't attract any official notice. I had to consciously resist the temptation to snake my Honda through traffic as if I were being chased. I still felt trapped. The gusting Santa Anas, in their second week, threw dirt devils across the road, and I accelerated through them all, breaking up the little tornadoes of dust and desert detritus. The sensation of bonds on my wrists was unbearable. At a stoplight I ripped my watch off my wrist and threw it as hard as I could against the passenger window, but it didn't make any difference. My grip on my hysteria was fast slipping, and I screeched into my own driveway not a moment too soon.

At home I felt safer. I bolted myself in and then tried to eat because I couldn't take my little silver pill on an empty stomach. All I could manage was a glass of milk before I swallowed the pill and then paced through the house, checking the windows.

Maybe this was a mental problem, not just the lack of sleep. Something was definitely unsettling in my mind. I dug in my desk until I came up with the business card for a local therapist my Berkeley therapist had given me. I decided that if I still felt bad in the morning I would call her.

When I started to feel groggy I went to bed.

The pill did its trick. I felt myself falling into unconsciousness, but for some reason I tried to fight it. I actually crawled off the bed onto the floor, trying to escape the clutches of the bedroom and the yawning darkness. I woke up halfway between the bed and the hallway about two hours later. Then I threw up everything I'd eaten for the last year.

I vomited—or tried to—for over an hour. Several times I felt as if I really was going to die. I sensed a chasm of emptiness near me, and part of me crawled toward it even while I gripped the toilet seat to keep from falling down.

After what seemed like an eternity, I rinsed my mouth and faced the task of cleaning up the mess I'd made. When I could lie down again, I was able to find enough humor to tell myself that I hadn't thought I could feel worse than I did with the headaches, and obviously I had tempted fate. Like people saying "You can't miss it" when they give you directions, and then of course you're in Key West when you were looking for Seattle.

"Okay," I muttered, "I can feel worse than this, there's no need to prove it to me." Then I went to sleep and immediately fell into the dreaming again.

I was resting. I floated. "I Honestly Love You" was running through my head.

Then something touched me, prodded me. In my dream, and in my bed, I opened my eyes. My dream eyes saw a misshapen, ghoulish face, and I screamed—in my dream, and in my bed. I would have sworn that the top of my head opened and my brain throbbed under an onslaught of explosive pain. The face disappeared. The lights went out.

The sensation was like nothing I'd ever felt. The closest comparison I can think of was when my mother had probed under the skin of my palm with a pin for a splinter that was festering. My brain felt like a pin was sifting through it.

The dream me was still screaming, and both of us were thrashing against bonds that held us immobile. Then the pain in my head abruptly stopped and the scream changed.

:HELP...ME...:

Holy shit. The relief from the pain stopping was so great I

started to laugh, and then I was crying because now I was hearing voices. A voice.

:HELP...ME...:

:HELP...ME...:

:HELP...ME...:

:HELP...ME...:

I didn't believe the voice was real. I'd had way too much therapy to believe it for even a minute. It sounded a little bit like my voice, as if I were talking inside my head to myself. But I knew I wasn't because I was thinking about what to do, not talking to myself.

:HELP...ME...:

:HELP...ME...:

I don't believe in possession. I don't read Stephen King novels. I never saw any Amityville movies or Halloween Part Twelve. *The X-Files* gives me the heebie-jeebies—I watched one episode and now I can't face oysters on the half shell. I think people who like to be scared and grossed out are slightly off the beam. But there was a voice in my head that I couldn't shut out. I felt pinned to my own bed, even though I wasn't, and I was physically bruised, battered, and depleted.

:HELP...ME...:

:HELP...ME...:

It wasn't something I ate unless someone slipped a psychedelic mushroom or peyote into my chow.

:HELP...ME...:

:HELP...ME...:

I didn't know what to do. Nothing in college had ever given me a clue about resisting voices in my head. Basic Sanity 101 hadn't been an elective for accounting majors, and it was *not* covered in the IRS handbook.

:HELP...ME...:

:HELP...ME...:

After about forty more help me's I got really pissed off. I mean who gave whatever was in my head the right to talk to me? Okay, all that therapy long ago might not have taught me how to handle voices in my head, but it had taught me how to redirect anger. Anger was not going to win. I thought as long and as hard as I could about tax code, and the voice got a lot fainter.

Hah. Whatever it was couldn't cope with the difference between a 501(c)(3) and a 501(c)(6).

:HELP...ME...:

Tax code is so boring I did manage to doze off while considering the different forms of depreciation available to a sole proprietorship. But then I dreamed again.

Chapter 2

A new dream.

I dreamed about being bounced like a rag doll in a boxcar. I couldn't use my arms and legs for balance or protection because they were weighed down. Or tied. My dream head felt as if it would split open, and there was no light anywhere. When I jolted out of the dream it was nearly two A.M. I turned on all the lights in the house and made myself a large pot of noodles with butter and Parmesan cheese. I stuffed myself as if I hadn't eaten in days, and a part of me still felt hungry.

The sensation of being bounced accompanied everything I did. Trying to move around felt a little bit like walking in an airplane during turbulence. When the sensation abruptly stopped I wasn't really surprised, just relieved. Even though I was pretty sure it wasn't a good thing, I was starting to get used to the dreams and their effect on me while I was awake.

I called in sick, assured supervisor Emily that I had seen a doctor, then kept my promise to myself about calling the local therapist. She seemed genuinely concerned, but said if I wanted to see her soon, it would have to be that day at lunchtime.

I wanted to take another pill and sleep the day away, but a

shower and something nutritious were necessary. I was leery of getting queasy again, so I made do with a glass of milk and several pieces of toast. I felt a little better by the time I left the house.

Corinna Metzger had an office in a small, run-down building just outside the fashionable circle of Fresno's main hospital district. I waited for a few minutes in a cozy chair, getting sleepy. When the receptionist said I could go in I wanted to press her snooze button, but she insisted on being perky.

"Julia, please sit down," Corinna said, after introducing herself. She was probably around five-four, and her hair was long, straight, and black with threads of silver.

"Thanks," I said, trying to hide my nerves. I had never liked going to see Janet Rebeau in Berkeley, even though I liked her and she had helped me tremendously. It was all so personal.

"Janet sent me a short note several years ago, letting me know she had given you my card. Janet and I go way back."

I was somewhat reassured. I hadn't relished going over my case history. "So you know something about me."

"Enough. I know that Janet thought you had come a long way in dealing with your anger and letting go. But why don't you tell me why you're here?"

"Well, I'm having nightmares. I hear...a woman calling out for help. I suddenly feel paranoid and like I'm being chased, or that I'm fainting, but I'm not. It's as if there are two of me."

Janet nodded. "And what do you think might be causing these nightmares?"

At least she hadn't asked me how it made me feel. "I don't know. Stress? I had a terrible migraine over the weekend."

"Did Janet ever talk to you about therapy maintenance?"

I thought about it. "No."

"Well, as much as members of my profession might not like my point of view, I've always held that therapy doesn't cure anything, that it just helps an individual deal with the source of the problem in a positive way instead of a self-destructive way. So—and we'd have to spend some time discovering if this is

19

true—maybe your earlier therapy is wearing off. Maybe you just need a booster shot."

Could be, I thought.

"Your adolescence was quite traumatic, so we'll also need to explore if this might be the emergence of new trauma that Janet and you never dealt with. Does this situation seem familiar? Or new?"

"A little of both," I said, confused.

"So we'll keep our options open as we talk. Have the receptionist schedule you for twice a week for the next month. We'll get to know each other and see where that leads us."

"Okay." What had I expected? One session would make me all better? Corinna didn't believe in cures, either. Hmm. I wasn't sure my budget could handle a therapist not determined to cure me. "Do you think we have a lot of work to do?"

"You tell me." Corinna had that smug therapist smile that I had always found irritating, even though Janet had claimed it was just my anger finding a near source.

"I don't know," I said.

"Well, if this isn't about your adolescence and we have to go earlier, this could take some time."

How early? Previous lives? Had I been a saloon madam or lady-in-waiting, and was that me now pissed off about the way her life had turned out? Forget it, I thought. This life is hard enough without digging up old ones.

I told the receptionist I'd call to make the appointments. I was going to have to think about it long and hard before I committed myself to more time on the couch. On the way back to the car, the wind tried to blow me over several times and I felt as if dust had seeped through my clothing. Fall in Fresno.

Home again, and feeling exhausted, I downed another pill and fell into murky sleep. I was dreaming, but all I could make out were darkness and a voice, very far away, calling out, but I didn't understand the words. I took another shower when I woke up. When I looked at myself in the bathroom mirror I told myself I wasn't seeing what I was seeing.

Carol called in the evening, just after I'd put *Wuthering Heights* into the VCR.

"Sweetie, I've got an herbalist that I really trust—you should go see her. I'm sure she could get you back on your feet."

"It's just something I ate," I said. "I made it worse by taking some medication on an empty stomach. I'll be at work tomorrow. I'm much better." All true, and all lies.

"Are you sure this isn't related to those headaches you had last weekend?"

I was sure it was related, but how could I tell Carol that? How could I tell her that my wrists and ankles were ringed with red and my chest itched like my ankles did when I wrapped them in runner's tape?

Carol finally left me in peace. The movie clunked into place in the VCR and moments later I was booting up my home computer. Mari's departure had given me plenty of time to explore cyberspace at night, and I'd rapidly become one of those people who believes if it can't be found on the Web it doesn't exist. Click, click, click and I was searching Yahoo for Web sites related to sleep disorders. Laurence Olivier brooded at Merle Oberon as I waded through the search process.

I still felt my problem was bad sleep. Bad sleep leads to hallucinations—I knew that from *Star Trek*—and the mind is a powerful thing, which explained the marks on my wrists and ankles. I told the dead plant on the windowsill that such things were not completely unheard of. They could even make rational, scientific sense.

Not only was I hallucinating, I was getting really good at lying to myself because there was nothing scientific about the voice.

Sometimes it was louder, sometimes it was completely silent. I know that I had heard it while I was sleeping, and if I let myself, I'd hear it now. "Crocodile Rock" was playing in the background of my mind.

I was distinctly aware that the part of me that could hear the voice was having a whale of an emotional ride. That part of me would feel anger, then fright, then utter despair, then hysteria. I suspected that if I slept all of me would feel these mood swings. The little silver pills were getting less effective, but I wasn't going to go back to a doctor until I'd done a little research myself.

The Yahoo search results were initially disappointing. Many of the Web sites turned out to be run by pharmaceutical companies, one of whom manufactured my little silver pills.

I finally worked my way down the search results to blogs and forums for posting and reading messages related to sleep disorders.

A hospital user group led me to an insomnia journal that had links to message boards for sufferers of sleep apnea, delayed-phase and restless leg syndrome. Were my legs restless? I could click to take a test and find out. Instead, I followed links, not sure what I was looking for. The sites where "awake at night" was interpreted as meaning "I want sex" were sleazy—I didn't want that kind of "sweet dreams." Parasites. I found a Live Journal apnea community with a few posts about dreams and sleeplessness from the last few days, but no one seemed to be describing quite what I was experiencing.

Then I struck pay dirt. It was a message titled, "Sleepless in the Central Valley." In it I read that an ongoing support group for people with sleep disorders met weekly on Saturday mornings. I e-mailed the address given for more info and within a few minutes received back an auto-responder message giving me the time and address of the meeting the day after tomorrow. It was right here in Fresno, but I'd have willingly driven to Bakersfield or even up to Modesto or Sacramento.

I felt as if I had done something positive to take control of the situation. I wasn't passively taking pills and calling in sick, hoping I'd wake up all cured.

I shut down my computer and took advantage of what I knew was a temporary absence of the voice to make oatmeal with brown sugar and cinnamon. It tasted so good I made myself a slice of cinnamon toast.

Feeling pleasantly sated, I curled up on the sofa with my favorite blanket and pillow and swapped out one Olivier movie for another. Joan Fontaine was a nervous ingénue who turned to pudding when Olivier brooded—and that man could brood. "You little fool" he called her, and she loved it. If I'd been more like Joan Fontaine I'm sure Mari and I would have lasted longer. It was my failing that being called a fool brought out the four- and five-letter words. This movie would be over if Joan Fontaine had retorted, "Listen you self-involved, poor little rich boy, get that painting of your dead wife off the wall or I'll take one of those family swords to it." But she didn't say that and so had a great romance. I'd called Mari a know-it-all bitch and now I was single. So much for the idea that relationships thrive when people talk.

For some reason, when I closed my eyes I could see swaying coral-tinted fronds in a gentle breeze and hear the soothing crash of the surf. Mingled with the surf was the lulling tune of "My Love."

If the dreams were all like this I wouldn't mind so much. I fell asleep just as Mrs. Danvers caressed Rebecca's underwear and explained to Joan Fontaine that it had been made by the nuns of Saint Claire.

I knew I was asleep. But I could also hear Laurence Olivier confessing that he'd hated Rebecca. I could still hear his voice even while, from inside my dream, I hummed along with, "The Way We Were."

Slowly, though, I was sliding more and more into the dream. It seemed to take a long time for me to fully settle into the dream, as if I had a distance to travel, or the little silver pill was slowing time. I finally slipped into what felt like a cold, damp well. I was in the dream again.

:*Help me.*:

"I'm not going to help you." I answered reflexively, before I remembered my staunch promise that I wouldn't do so, because

23

that would mean I was talking to myself in dreams.

The pin-sifting sensation came back, but not nearly as painful as before. It wasn't exactly pleasant, either.

:*Help me.*:

"Why should I?"

:*They kill.*:

"Kill you?" Oh stop it, Maddy, I told myself. Don't encourage this hallucination. You'll only make it believe it's real.

:*Poison.*:

Well, that accounted for all the throwing up. Wait a minute, who are we talking about here? Who is we? Julia Madison, there is only you here. Stop talking to yourself.

:*Help me.*:

"Stop it. You're making me nuts."

:*Nuts.*:

Visions of filberts, almonds, pecans, walnuts, pistachios, pines and peanuts floated through my head at random. I wasn't really thinking about them, but there they were and then the faintest hint of pin-sifting stopped.

:*Perceive you do not want...be made nuts. Will...cease.*:

In a wink it was all gone. The voice, the pin-sifting, all the terror and anger and pain. Only my sense of being both awake and asleep was left. "Where did you go?"

Nothing.

Great, I thought. I was aware that I rolled over to settle more deeply into sleep, and aware that while the voice had stopped I was still caught in the dream. I could just hear the closing bars of "The Way We Were."

I put in a long day on Friday to catch up with a lot of files. I made brisk phone calls to delinquent taxpayers—none of whom wanted to talk to me—and efficiently marked off my progress calculating revised tax settlements. Long after everyone else had left I worked in the silent office, taking pleasure from the routine of the work and my ability to do it as competently and quickly as ever. It was comforting to know that one thing hadn't changed.

The voice was as good as its word—it was gone. It was fairly easy to ignore the other intrusions; ripples of fear and anger were the most common. Several times I thought the fluorescent lights had either flared or dimmed when they hadn't, and a variety of songs played in my head—everything from "Superfly" to "Delta Dawn." Whoever was in charge of the dial had eclectic tastes.

Whatever the problem was, why ever I couldn't sleep—it was under control. But I still planned on going to the sleep disorder support group in the morning because I wanted more than "under control." I wanted to be back the way I had been before, every inch the boring, paralyzed, and mostly hopeless person I knew myself to be. I hadn't realized until now that I valued that Julia Madison somewhat. Certainly more than the Julia who heard voices, who was in danger of turning into the "Maddy" her mother had chided so often for having a high orbit when it came to reality. She had never liked my ability to slip into what she called "Maddy's land of make-believe."

My mother called herself a practical person, and she spent most of her life getting by day to day. Today mattered: the future did not. She had tried to beat out of me any view of the world other than hers. She did succeed in making me realize that the world is usually a hostile place, but had failed in most other ways.

When I got home there was a message from her on the machine. Odd that I had been thinking of her, something I don't often do, and that she should call.

Even someone without my years of experience at it would have heard the bourbon in her cigarette-ravaged voice. She gushed with affection and a desire to see her little girl, but bus fare had gone up and she couldn't quite make the ticket. Any veil there might have been on her request for money was completely removed by her assuring me she hadn't moved.

I wrote her a check for two hundred dollars and walked it to the mailbox. She'd never buy the bus ticket, and with any luck she wouldn't call for at least two months. Two hundred would last a long time in Vegas when you waited just enough tables to make the trailer park rent, played just enough poker to get free drinks, and were just friendly enough to other players to get free meals and a comfortable bed in an air-conditioned hotel most nights.

I was getting ready for bed when the background noise in my head got louder. I could hear Maureen McGovern crooning "The Morning After," a song I hadn't heard in ages and hadn't much liked the first time around.

Little silver pill, come to momma, I thought. I fell asleep in short order and dreamed about my knee surgery, or something like it. Grogginess, an IV in my arm, fingers being pricked, being wheeled and moved, and mostly just drifting with no sense of the deep dark of night.

My radio alarm woke me with a nice Mozart sonata. I'm not Mozart's biggest fan, but it was delightful compared to the retro junk I had been hearing in my head. Maybe, I suddenly thought, my fillings were picking up a radio station or something. That could explain everything. Except my fillings are all resin, not silver or gold, and I hadn't had any dental work in years.

I wasn't sure if my head radio was playing anything, but I cranked up Bach's Double Concerto in D Minor just to make sure I didn't hear it if it was. Feeling fairly civilized I slipped into jeans after my shower and pulled the cleanest of my long-sleeved polo shirts over my head. It had a small Eeyore embroidered on the pocket. Mari hadn't thought it at all funny when I'd told her Eeyore was my personal god.

The support group met in a classroom at Valley High. The drive from southwest to northeast Fresno takes about twenty minutes most of the time, but, with the Santa Anas in full blast, speeds on Highway 99 were slower as motor homes and big rigs swayed in the viciously unpredictable crosswind.

Maybe this was all just the Santa Anas. Different groups had been researching the psychological impact of the Santa Ana winds for years. The suicide rate went up, crime and domestic violence skyrocketed. Add the ninety-plus temperature during the fall windy season and all of southern California from Malibu to Barstow became a tinderbox, figuratively and literally.

My little Honda handled the wind pretty well. My driving was much better when there was no little voice in my head. I found the right classroom with no problem and felt immediately relieved that almost everyone there was female. I prefer the company of women. I might not be the purist or separatist that Marigold Jane Tempest was, but I still think women are just plain smarter and usually more interesting than men. I'm sexist that way. So sue me.

I started to slide into a desk near the back of the room, but a woman I assumed was the group leader waved me forward.

"Please sit closer. I'm just handing out copies of the bibliography on SDS that Vina put together."

I took the stapled pages and smiled a hello to my neighbors as I sat down. The bibliography read "Sleep Disorder Syndrome Et Cetera" across the top.

"It's always nice to have a new face," the leader was saying. "We had two new people last week."

I glanced around the room—there were about eleven or twelve total.

"It's the Santa Anas," the woman next to me said. She had short-cropped black hair that resembled a Marine chop-top, but it accentuated amazing cheekbones. Her dark brown skin was a few shades lighter than Marigold's. I was wallpaper paste pale next to her.

The woman who was apparently the group leader responded, "You could be right, JT." She couldn't have been more than five-one in her modest pumps and I thought idly that she was probably wearing weights to keep from blowing away, like the Flying Nun. "Well, everybody, I'm Geri, the convener of our support group for this month. Next month Rose is going to take over"—she nodded toward a redhead on the other side of the room—"and after that we'll need a volunteer. It's pretty easy duty, so please think about it.

"For our newcomer, the format is pretty simple. We'll spend the first fifteen to twenty minutes on new symptoms. With the Santa Anas I think we'll all have something to say. Then we have about a half hour of mingling, where the people who seem to have similar symptoms can talk together. After that we have book and medical journal reports on medication and new treatments. There are never enough people willing to do this, and there's still lots of undigested material, so please consider volunteering to read for the group, okay? Just because Vina can get us all the material doesn't mean she should read it for us, too. Okay." She inhaled finally. "JT, maybe you'd like to start. You already mentioned that this week had been really tough."

JT was nodding. "Remember last Saturday I said I thought I was staying in REM too long? I still feel that way, like I'm skipping right over all the other stages and falling right into dream state. My nightly sleep is down—I used to manage four hours, and now I'm just barely making three."

Geez, that made my five or so hours—broken though they usually were—seem like paradise. I made a mental note to talk to her during the mingle time, because she had mentioned dreams.

"Who wants to go next?"

There was a silence, then Rose said, with a really attractive Irish accent, "I really think the Santa Anas are working everybody over. My sleep problem, for the newer people, is panic waking. When I come up to light sleep I wake up in a panic instead of going to sleep again. I usually wake up with some sort of picture in my head almost like a snapshot. This past week the pictures have been really vivid and somewhat frightening, so going back to sleep is even harder."

After that everyone seemed eager to share. People gave their names and described what was different for them this week. Most attributed some or all of the change to the Santa Anas. I realized that I was probably going to end up last because I was listening so hard. It seemed as if some of the other women were experiencing a portion of what I was, but no one had quite the same combination of problems. Rose had panic attacks from vivid mental images. JT was dreaming more deeply than usual. Vina was experiencing mood swings and night sweats—though she readily said she was in menopause and it could be hormones.

I was last, and Geri nodded encouragingly. "I'm Julia," I began. "I've never had trouble sleeping before. Now that I've had a chance to listen to everybody, I'm pretty sure that the problems started a couple of days after the winds came up. I've had really vivid dreams. Sounds, images, feelings, more intense than any movie. And headaches. And nausea. They all come and go."

I stopped and decided not to mention the skin rashes I'd had last week. My polo shirt covered the red rings on my wrists. "What's even weirder is that I keep hearing music, like a radio station from my past is playing all the songs I've ever heard."

Geri's gaze went from sympathetic listener to laser intensity.

I swallowed and went on. "I got a sleeping pill prescription that did help me sleep, but the other stuff hasn't really stopped. I don't want to get addicted to the pills, and I'm open to nontraditional stuff." Other people had mentioned meditation, acupuncture, acupressure and herbal remedies as helping to moderate different stages of sleep. "I just want to feel like I'm controlling it instead of it controlling me."

Geri laughed. "Don't we all? Thank you for sharing Julia. Thank you everybody. Let's mingle."

JT turned to me. "Have you ever remembered your dreams before?"

I shook my head. "Rarely."

"I was never aware before that I was dreaming. I know I must have been, but I never remembered before. But now they're so intense they're waking me up."

Geri sat down at the desk in front of me. "What kind of songs?"

"Mostly pop stuff."

She chewed on her lip for a minute. I noticed that Rose had come up behind Geri. "Go ahead and tell her," she urged Geri. "It can't hurt, and it's what we're here for."

Geri gave Rose a rueful smile. "I'm not used to being thought crazy."

"Not like me," Rose said, her voice full of teasing. She sat down in front of JT and held out her hand to me. "Rose O'Day, bona fide sleep psychic. If I could do what I do in my sleep while I was awake I'd be rich."

I shook her hand, not sure what to think.

She grinned. "I don't have to be psychic to know that you're wondering what you've let yourself in for."

"Stop teasing the poor woman, Rose." Geri's arm twitched as if she were going to reach toward Rose. Aha, I thought. They know each other very well.

"Go ahead and tell her. I believe you. Give someone else a chance."

JT looked as confused as I felt.

Geri gave up chewing her lip and said, "I'm hearing music all the time. It started a few days ago. Especially when I'm asleep. Usually when I wake up I'm like Rose—in a total panic. Lately I wake up singing to myself."

Two weeks ago I wouldn't have believed a word she said. After a moment's concentration I could make out a tune in the back of my mind. "Are you hearing anything now?"

She didn't even hesitate. "Sure am. Paul Simon. The end of 'Loves Me Like a Rock.'"

I must have gone pretty pale because JT asked, "Are you okay?"

I nodded with an effort. "Just major league creeped out. Know what I mean?" To Geri I said, "It started a few days ago—Wednesday?"

She nodded. She looked creeped out, too.

Rose looked at someone behind me. "How's the other group

doing, Vina?"

I realized that the participants had divided into two groups, and the only men were in the other group. Most of them, if I remembered right, had medical reasons for sleep disorders, like the man who had phantom limb pain that had never faded from the loss of his right arm.

Vina sat on the desk next to Rose. Her posture was perfect. "They're already discussing the new study in the *New England Journal of Medicine* about delta stage and pain." She spoke with precisely modulated tones.

JT was still studying me. "Why don't we give Julia a little history of the group?"

Geri nodded. "I think that would be helpful."

JT continued, "The four of us met in this group over the past two years. We all have basic sleep pattern disturbance and found that our problems...and lives...well, matched. So we've gotten close."

They're all lesbians, I suddenly thought. Just like me. "I understand," I said, looking meaningfully from Rose to Geri. Living in Fresno hones the gaydar to a fine edge. I knew I was right.

"We keep this support group going even though now that we've found each other we don't really need it," Vina added. Of the four of us she looked least like my image of a lesbian. On the other hand, she looked like a librarian, and I've known plenty of lesbian librarians—a militant bunch for all their ladylike airs. "It has helped new people a lot just being here, but we could do this in a chat room just as easily."

"But then I'd never get to see you in the flesh," JT said. "And lord knows Rose and Geri hardly come up for air."

Rose blushed instantly and deeply as only a redheaded Irish woman can. Geri remained utterly composed.

Just to make sure they knew that I understood, I said, "Are we talking newlyweds here?"

Vina shared a relieved smile with JT. "And how."

In the back of my mind, quite divorced from the good feeling I always got when I met new lesbians in Fresno, was a ripple of panic. Geri and I were hearing the same music. It must have been a lucky guess, I told myself. It was just a lucky guess because if it weren't it meant a whole lot of stuff I thought was rubbish might be true.

Rose's blush faded as quickly as it had come. "Maybe this is all just the winds."

"I could believe that," Vina said. "I've been going through the change for a year now. These recent hot flashes are the most severe I've ever had. I felt as if I was going to sweat to death one night. And the mood swings are equally distressing. Two or three nights ago I woke up crying my eyes out, and I had no idea why."

Me, the real me, not the dream me, the real Julia Madison, panicked. My heart was racing, and I wanted to get the hell out of there before anyone said anything more.

"You okay?" JT was looking at me with concern again.

This time I shook my head. I looked at Geri. "'Tie a Yellow Ribbon Round the Old Oak Tree.'"

She visibly gulped.

"Holy shit," JT said.

There was a long silence, and I studied my socks intensely.

Finally Rose said, "You know what I would like to do? I'd like us to go back to our place where we can talk a little more openly. I think...we need to talk."

Vina reached across and touched my arm. "Stop thinking you've lost your mind."

My gaze suddenly focused on Vina's wrist. There was a faint red band of irritation all the way around it. I glanced at her other wrist. It matched.

My stomach heaved. As calmly as possible, I asked, "Which way is the bathroom?"

"I'll show you," JT said.

I followed her to the hallway. "Hurry, please," I said. "I think

I'm going to be sick."

JT took my arm and broke into a run. "It's just up here."

I just made it. It was official. I'd thrown up more in the last week than in my entire life, and that included the Annie Green Springs and aspirin episode.

JT was amazing. She rubbed my back when I finally subsided, then brought me wet paper towels.

"I'm so embarrassed," I finally mumbled.

"Don't worry," she said. "I'm a nurse. I'm used to just about every fluid that comes out of the human body. Or a cat's for that matter."

She helped me to my feet and over to the sink where I splashed more water on my face. "What brought that on?"

I wiped my face raw with the scratchy brown paper towels. "Fear, I think. Did you see the marks on Vina's wrists?"

She nodded and looked at me curiously. Then I pulled back the cuffs of my shirt and showed her my wrists. She swallowed hard, just like Geri had.

Chapter 3

"I know better than anyone that these kind of phenomena aren't in the medical journals." JT was partially propped up on large pillows on the floor in Rose and Geri's small, tidy living room. She looked comfortable. "But that doesn't mean they don't exist."

Rose sipped her iced tea, and I envied her apparent calm. She seemed quite used to unusual things happening inside her head. "You don't have to convince me, J-girl. I'm Irish for starts. I believe in leprechauns, and I mean the ones who'll lead you into a bog so you starve to death. During the worst panic over the plague there were hundreds of documented cases of spontaneous stigmata. People would develop vivid bruising or even bleeding in their palms and feet in the traditional crucifixion pattern."

"Don't get religious on me," Vina said curtly. She had admitted to feeling flutters of anger, flutters which I felt as well.

"Religious obsession sometimes masks mental illness and vice versa," Rose said. "It's just an example. Hey, stress can make your hair fall out, right? So why wouldn't intense emotion explain skin rashes and markings?"

Even though I felt substantially fortified by my quick stop at

Mickey D's on the way to this house shared by Geri and Rose, I didn't have the energy to argue with Rose. She obviously believed what she said. "I'm not intensely emotional—not usually. What I am doing is dreaming of being confined." I held out my wrists. "And these are the marks of the bonds. I don't know why it's happening, and I have no idea why Vina has these marks, too."

"Me, neither," said Rose. "But something intense is happening in both your dreams. I don't see that it's impossible for these marks to derive from deeply experienced dreams."

"That would mean we're having the same dream," Vina said. "Twin phenomena is the only time I've ever heard of shared dreams."

If anyone said phenomena again I was going to explode. Next we'd be calling the Ghostbusters. "But lately, well, since taking the sleeping pills, I haven't been experiencing the dreams vividly. If anything I have more emotional distance, not less." I was getting that creeped-out feeling again and starting to wonder just how crazy Rose was.

Geri stirred in the depths of the large, comfy sofa and said, "'The Night the Lights Went Out in Georgia.'"

"Shit." Every time I would think that I should get back in my car and drive home Geri would mention whatever song was in her head. I think she knew how close I was to bolting. "Look. I know you're all trying to help me—"

"Help you?" JT rolled her expressive, deep brown eyes. "Honey, I want to help me here. And I'm sure that Geri wishes that damn radio would shut off. And Rose would like to go back to her ordinary psychic dreaming, whatever that is. Vina's got a reason to solve this puzzle, too. I don't mean to be rude, but this is not just about you."

"I'm sorry," I said, chastened. "I don't mean to be so self-centered."

"It's easy to do." Rose gently patted my knee. "You do seem to be the focus here. You're getting the whole picture."

"It's a picture that doesn't make any sense at all."

Rose's sympathetic smile turned confident. "I think I know someone who can help with that."

Geri sat up. "Shandra?"

"Yeah, Shandra."

JT bit back a yawn. "Now why did I know we'd be off to see the wizard before long?"

Geri laughed. "She's not a wizard. She's not even a witch. She's an adept."

What the fuck was an *adept*?

This was all getting too weird, too fast.

One of the reasons I moved to Fresno was its status as a plain, old ordinary place. I'd lived in an Aptos trailer park growing up, but it was still the Bay Area, and my undergraduate business degree was from Berkeley. You could walk across campus on any given day and see at least a half dozen people in one esoteric garb or another.

After burning myself out in the consulting branch of a big accounting firm, and dating too many women who always talked about getting in touch with their feelings and never did until they were screaming at me, I had wanted a down-to-earth, homey place like Fresno. When my number came up on the IRS hiring list, I jumped at the chance. I didn't care about the heat or the smell when the breeze drifted from the stockyards. About ninety minutes in the car and I could be at the foot of El Capitan in Yosemite. Until this year, I had reveled in the grape orchards and fall colors and been happy that I would eventually turn into a raisin. I knew the future of my life in Fresno, and that feeling of control had been welcome.

I certainly hadn't expected to meet someone like Marigold Jane Tempest in Fresno. She was like a piece of Berkeley, and I think that's what attracted me to her in the first place—holistic, politically correct in everything, all-natural, all-cotton and wired for if-it-feels-good-do-it sex. Through Mari I'd become slightly acquainted with the feminist spirituality community in Fresno—small, but fervent. But I'd never expected that my own business would bring me into contact with an occult underworld. Adepts? Witches? What next, *I Dream of Jeannie*?

JT was laughing at something Geri said, and I tried to return to the conversation. I couldn't ignore the sirens of warning going off in my head, but neither could I find it in me to get up and leave.

Rose returned from the other room. "Shandra can see us this afternoon if everyone's up to it. She had a cancellation."

Apparently, we were all up to it. I accepted JT's offer of a lift, and off we went—as JT kept saying—to see the wizard.

Even now I wonder what would have happened if I'd just said no.

There are no haunted mansions in Fresno, but I was still surprised when we pulled up in front of a very ordinary looking tract home about halfway between Fresno and Clovis. I had expected something spookier, something more *Rocky Horror*.

Shandra turned out to be even mousier than I was, with middling brown hair and a bit of a tummy where I was bony. I considered myself pretty forgettable, but I knew I could have seen Shandra a hundred times and never remembered her.

I thought that until she looked me right in the eyes. Her not blue nor brown nor green eyes had a depthless quality that was disconcerting. She shook my hand while making piercing eye contact, and I saw her gold-ringed irises contract and widen as she studied me.

Rose took charge of explaining what we were all experiencing together and separately, but the whole time Shandra studied me. She would glance at the others when they were mentioned, and she briefly examined Vina's and my wrists, but mostly she stared at me. I found it difficult not to blush.

As Rose's narrative tailed off, Shandra reached for my hand. I hesitated and then relented. Unless this was some sort of cult initiation, I couldn't think how I might be harmed. I had absolutely no idea where any of this was heading.

"You've traveled The Road recently," she said.

"The Road." I glanced at Rose who smiled slightly and not particularly reassuringly. "I drive to work."

Shandra's intensity dissolved into a hearty laugh. She let go of my hand. "Okay, you really are a neophyte."

"I'm not just a clueless newbie," I said. "I'm a doubting Thomas." I tried and failed to maintain eye contact.

She reached for my hand again. Her palm was warm and smooth. "The Road is another plane. People who are sensitive to reality beyond the five senses can sometimes travel The Road to find helpers, talk to other travelers, sometimes call souls that have passed beyond. And sometimes they're just fooling themselves. But you've been on The Road recently. Your aura is shimmering with its energy."

Poppycock. I wanted to say it, but I didn't. Shandra smirked, and I knew she'd heard me anyway.

"You don't consider yourself psychically gifted, do you?"

"Ah, no," I said firmly. "Not in the least."

She let go of my hand. "Can I ask you some questions?" I nodded, and she sat back in her chair. "Do you finish other people's sentences for them?"

"I try not to. It can be really annoying."

She arched her eyebrows slightly. "When you were growing up—just becoming a teenager maybe—do you remember being able to tell when someone was mad? Or afraid? Or going to hurt you?"

Everyone else in the room faded away. It was just Shandra and me. I nodded slowly. "I could always tell when my mom was going to get drunk. But that's not unusual for a child of an alcoholic parent." I blinked away ephemeral tricks of light, seeming strands of cool blue ribbons running between Shandra and me.

"There's more, isn't there?"

"I could always tell when men wanted me, um...I mean sexually. From the time I was about twelve or so. I knew when my mom's latest boyfriend was just waiting for her to leave." My jaw quivered. "I dealt with all this in therapy about fifteen years ago. That's not why I'm here."

"I know," Shandra said. "I'm not a therapist. But you knew when these men were predatory."

Tears started in my eyes. "I'd stay out all night. I knew where to hide. I wouldn't come home until my mom did. She'd whip me for it, but that was always easier to bear than getting caught by one of them. The times she'd hook up with a guy who wasn't interested in me were probably the happiest times in my entire adolescence."

"How about in adult relationships?"

"You mean knowing..." She nodded. "Only with men. I can never tell with women. I often wish I could, it would have saved me a few more years of therapy." Another attempt at a joke failed miserably. Tough room.

"You prefer women?" Shandra arched an eyebrow and swept all five of us with her incredible gaze. "That's interesting. You realize you all have a common bond, don't you?"

"That's just a coincidence," JT said. "We have no idea what other people might be experiencing."

I added, "It's easier for me to trust other lesbians. Birds of a feather."

Shandra just nodded and pursed her lips. "Tell me, do any ex-lovers have similar-sounding complaints about you?"

I blinked away tears and tried to laugh. "Yeah. I don't put any energy into the relationship, that's a big one."

"How about putting words in their mouth? Misreading their intentions?"

I thought about it. "Well, doesn't everyone argue about that? It would make me crazy when Mari would say she wasn't mad about something when it was obvious she was. Or she would say she liked something because it was PC when I could tell she didn't." We'd fought for three hours over a Women's Art project that had passed through town. I had thought it was crap on a dais and she had claimed she liked it. But I'd known—I'd just

39

known—she didn't like it any more than I did, but she wouldn't admit it.

"You're *sensitive*," Shandra pronounced. "Many people are and never know it. They put it down to good instincts. But you can tap into other people's emotions. Like a lie detector. And mostly they don't appreciate it."

"Right." I shook myself back to the present and realized the others were intently following our exchange. "Now if I only looked like Counselor Troi I could be in the movies."

Shandra frowned. "I'm trying to help."

"I know. I just find it hard to believe."

Rose leaned forward. "What about The Road? As soon as you said it I realized that she might be picking up something from someone on The Road."

Shandra was nodding. "That's what I was going to suggest we explore. Because there is something happening on The Road. A lot of random energy spilling over in an erratic pattern. I can't focus on the source. I know other people are trying to focus on it, but no one is sure quite what's up." She looked at me. "But you know."

Hah. I felt so skeptical that I couldn't find anything to say. I sneaked a glance at JT and was somewhat heartened to see a "whatever" expression on her face.

"You don't have anything to lose," Rose said.

"Except my dignity."

JT suddenly leaned forward. "Julia, dignity was not high on your card this morning. I don't believe in this any more than you do. But none of us are going to think you're being foolish if you take a look. Then you can rule it out."

I flushed, remembering how I had puked my guts out just because Vina had marks on her wrists like mine. Any remaining shred of dignity I had was not worth preserving if it would ease my sleep and get rid of "Touch Me in the Morning" now playing in my head.

"What would be involved?" I sensed Rose relaxing.

"Nothing but what we're already doing. But I'll help you go into a light trance, which will be nothing more than feeling as if you're awake and dreaming at the same time."

"I'm halfway there all the time lately," I said, trying to make it sound like yet another joke and with just as much success.

Shandra straightened. "Your dreams are with you right now?"

"Well, I don't know about with me at the moment. But if I concentrate a little it's almost like I'm falling asleep."

"Show me." Shandra's tone was so terse I didn't think of disobeying.

I closed my eyes, took a deep breath, and honed in on "Touch Me in the Morning." As I did I could feel the phantom bonds on my wrists and ankles. The itchy feeling came back to my chest. I began to swim through emotional tides—despair, longing and... loneliness.

I heard Shandra catch her breath, but it was now very far away. Hands, probably hers, rested lightly on my shoulders. From the hands came a soothing warmth, encouragement and a sense of courage. I went as deeply toward the dream as I did when sleeping, yet I was still awake.

I became aware of a steady beep. It was a familiar sound because of its regular rhythm. Its tone clashed badly with the new song, "You're So Vain." There was a moment of disorientation, then,

:Help me.:

From Shandra I sensed a swelling rush of wonder, then prompting. She said, probably to Rose, "That didn't take long. I wonder if she's close by?"

"Who are you?" I spoke aloud, and my distant senses felt the others jump in surprise.

:Help me.:

"Where are you?"

:No nuts.:

I laughed out loud. "I'm probably mad as a hatter, but we may as well talk."

41

The pin-sifting feeling abruptly returned. It was as if multiple movie screens had opened in my mind's eye and images spilled and blinked over them faster than I could track. One screen was filling up with fedoras, bowlers, baseball caps, sun visors, Barbra Streisand's ostrich feathers in *Hello Dolly* and all the fantastical headgear from a long-ago production of *Beach Blanket Babylon*. Another screen prominently featured Olivia de Havilland in *The Snake Pit*. She turned into Big Nurse, then Jack Nicholson with an axe, and then my mother. That's when I panicked.

"Stop that!" I tried to stand up, but Shandra held me in my chair.

I felt myself rising out of the dream. I wasn't sure I could call it a dream anymore. I became more and more aware of Shandra and the others, and the movie screens faded away.

:Return.:

I was pierced with a wave of such emptiness and longing that my eyes teared. I offered the only comfort I had.

"I'll try."

With a popping sensation I straightened up. Shandra was leaning heavily on the chair. Vina was wiping away a tear, while Rose and Geri were virtually dancing with curiosity. JT was looking at me as if I'd grown a second head.

That's when I fainted.

"I feel responsible," JT said for the fiftieth time.

"I did eat something."

"You should have had a large glass of juice, not a Happy Meal."

"I had orange soda," I said.

JT gave me the look that remark deserved, and then went searching through my refrigerator for acceptable replenishment-type food. I'd never been fond of food as medicine, but JT was apparently much like Mari in that way.

"I'm fine," I repeated.

JT humphed, then turned from the refrigerator with a carton

of milk, egg substitute, Parmesan cheese and leftover Boston Market chicken.

"Shandra said you should have a lot of protein. Traveling on The Road is very draining."

"Are you saying you believe in that stuff now?"

JT looked up from a mixing bowl I'd forgotten I owned. "No. I don't believe in it. But you went somewhere in your head, and wherever that somewhere was Vina was somehow there too."

Vina had described the same ache of loneliness I had felt. Our marks had mutually deepened and so had the pain.

JT's omelet tasted really good, and she was mollified that I asked for seconds. Her crisp military bearing was softened by the apron and I couldn't help but muse that there was something very sexy about a butch woman who could cook. I did the dishes while she talked about her life as a nurse. Thankfully, she said, she didn't have to be back on shift until tomorrow around noon.

"If you don't mind, if it's not an imposition, I'd like to sleep on your sofa tonight." She said it hesitantly, as if she was afraid I'd think she was angling for sleeping in my bed.

"I don't need nursing..." I began, not sure what to say.

"I know, it's more for me. I've been wondering if I slept in proximity to you if I'd have a better chance of remembering what I'm dreaming. Maybe it's the same dreams as you're having, just much less intense. I want to remember them. If it's got nothing to do with what you're dreaming I need to know."

I deliberated for a couple of seconds. "The sofa is yours," I said. My body—which never knows its own limits—chided me for not offering my bed. I was in no shape for sex no matter how long it had been since I'd had any and no matter how attractive JT was to my eyes.

"Thank you," JT said.

We talked for a while longer, then JT watched while I went online. Shandra had suggested that we check out www.magick. net for posts related to The Road. I thought it was pointless, but JT persuaded me it couldn't hurt.

The message board at that site had a lot of postings. A long thread of posts and responses to an original message titled "Lost Soul on The Road" was somewhat interesting. The original poster speculated that a recently deceased person was resisting the "natural turn of the wheel" and wandered, looking for his or her loved ones.

I was not particularly enthused with the idea that I was talking to a dead person in my head. I'd seen *Ghost*. Whoopi Goldberg is cute, but I have never aspired to be her or any role she has ever played.

A while after sundown I turned in. JT said she wouldn't go to sleep for hours, and as I left her she was checking her own mail.

I expected to lie awake for a while, wondering about what had happened today, but instead dropped off fairly quickly. I recognized that I was eager to go back to the voice and keep my promise.

It wasn't difficult to focus in on "Reelin' in the Years." Was I traveling on some sort of road? I didn't know. I was not aware of anyone else, just the music, and then the source of the voice.

:*Back.*:

Gratitude. I knew I smiled in my sleep. To be so welcome felt good.

"I promised."

:*Thank you.*:

"What is it like where you are?"

:*Cold.*:

The pin-sifting sensation was back. It was very gentle, but definitely there.

:*I prisoner. I captive.*:

"Why?"

:*Different. No defenses.*:

She—for I suddenly accepted that it was a she—moved. I could feel the weight of her bonds on my wrists and ankles. My chest felt sticky and itchy, like duct tape or something equally noxious was stuck to it.

"This is really unpleasant," I admitted.

:Tell me about it.:

The tone was so wry and like my own that I laughed.

:What is that?:

"What?"

:That...:

The pin-sifting sensation came back, but this time it wasn't even unpleasant. In my mind's eye I saw Carol and Mari laughing, heard the combined laughter of a theater audience, and even felt another chortle building up in my throat.

:Oh. Thank you.:

"What did you just do?"

:Don't...I...don't speak English very well. I...needed definitions.:

"And you took them right out of my head. That's kind of handy." Actually, I was rather annoyed. I mean this might still turn out to be just a dream, but sifting around in someone else's brain is rather cheeky.

:I am sorry. I don't mean to be...cheeky. But I must learn.:

"Stop that!" How rude, I thought. Reading other people's mind without their permission was against the rules of *Star Trek*, my official guide to the galaxy of weird.

:I am sorry. But I can't help it.:

"Don't I get any privacy?"

:Privacy?:

More sifting sensations.

:I see. I am not used to privacy where I come from.:

"Just where are you from?"

:You've never heard of it.:

"Try me. I read a lot." Sifting again, but the feeling was so faint that I might have missed it. What I noticed was that the movie screens were back. One flashed with images of Earth's continents, looking a little fuzzy in the Southern Hemisphere (I'd never learned that part very well), while another spilled over with special effects from *Star Trek* movies. Then they all fused together in one big screen where different cities and landscapes pulsed so rapidly I only recognized a few. But they were all places I'd been. A flicker of the rundown trailer park I'd grew up in was the last image, and then the screen in my head went blank.

:You have not read about my home. Your English might say it as Pallas.:

"You're right, I've never heard of it. Is it in Greece?" All I could relate Pallas to was the goddess Athena.

:No. You do not know where it is.:

The pain of it was, she did know I didn't know. "It's not really fair," I said. "You get to sift through me and I can't sift through you."

:I am not sure it would reverse. I have the skills for the distance between us. You would have to be closer.:

"Skills? Like what."

My mental screen lit up with The Amazing Kreskin, headlines about Jeanne Dixon's latest psychic predictions, and then it blanked out.

:You do not know yourself. You are on the surface of your...cortex.:

"I'm starting to get it. You're just a figment of my imagination exorcising some leftover crappola that Marigold snuck into my subconscious."

:Marigold? Figment? Exorcising? Crappola?:

All the movie screens lit up. Fantasy people I'd only dreamed up. Linda Blair spewing pea soup. Marigold flowers. My Marigold, laughing. Kneading bread. Chopping vegetables. Fucking me.

I tried to blank out the screen of Marigold leaning over me, her fingers deep and me urging her deeper. I writhed in embarrassment.

:Fucking?:

"That's very personal. Private. Oh..."

The screen expanded until I was the center of it. I dropped into my most sensuous moments, the sound of moans and gasps, cooing and begging all around me. The screen washed with crimson and indigo and then Marigold was whispering, "Oh god, Julieeee, eatmeeatmeeatmeeatme..."

46

My heart was racing, and I felt a searing heat between my legs. I tried to shut off the screen, but...she...was spilling my memories of sex and orgasms and foreplay and breasts and labia and clits and rubbing and hard and slick and salty and gasping, gasping, gasping all running through my mind, my body, it had been so long, it felt so good, so good...

:So good...:

"Julia."

:So good...:

"Julia!"

I woke up in a panic, suddenly realizing how Rose must feel every night. I hoped Vina had felt nothing of that.

JT was leaning over me. "You were moaning."

"Were you asleep?"

She nodded. "I think you woke me up, but I'm not sure. I was dreaming about a woman and I heard a woman's voice."

I bit my lower lip and sat up once I'd made sure my T-shirt covered all the parts it should. "That's probably her then. I think—I'm ready to admit that there's someone on the other end. A woman. She says she's being held prisoner."

JT studied me. "Did she say where she was?"

"No. But she—somehow she reads my mind—oh..."

"What? What is it?"

I closed my eyes. The feeling of panic had faded, and now I was aware that She, the dream woman, was back in my head.

:I frightened you. I am sorry.:

"It's okay," I said.

"She's back?" JT sat down on the bed.

I nodded at JT.

"Ask her where she is."

"She doesn't know."

:You helped make this more bearable. I had forgotten that there is more than pain.:

I blushed. "Don't mention it. It's kind of embarrassing that you saw it."

"Did that come from her?" JT shifted on the bed.

"What?"

"The images of...well, it was sexual."

"Oh. You sensed that?"

"I was dreaming about a woman, not someone I know."

"Was she black? With cornrows and two silver earrings in each ear?"

JT nodded, her eyes wide.

"Um, that's my ex."

JT whistled silently. "That was not a dream, but something that really happened?"

"Not all at once." I squirmed again, this time at the awareness of JT's warm body. I was also starting to feel drowsy.

"I've always wanted to go back to a dream exactly where I left off." JT stood up, and I was half relieved.

"Wouldn't that be nice?"

JT rubbed her arms. "Too much to hope for."

I couldn't help myself. "It seemed that good?"

She looked down at me, and her gaze slid over my face and then down my shoulders to my breasts. "If I was dreaming I was you, then you were a lucky woman."

I was short of breath. She was staring at my breasts and I was staring at hers.

I don't remember who did or said what next. What I do remember is that her mouth tasted of cinnamon and she smelled faintly of her leather jacket.

She cupped my face and kissed me thoroughly. Lingeringly. My head fell back, I fell back, she was on top of me, and together we shrugged out of our clothes. Her skin was warm against mine. It felt real, solid, not in the least like a dream.

"Oh." Her teeth found my nipples. I felt in my head the echo of my gasp.

:Oh.:

I was swamped with need, more than my own after a long spell of no one to hold me. Need and desire swam up through my mind. The movie screens came back. Mari was there again, her breasts against my mouth, my hands full of her hair, clutching her to me. Most prominent was what JT was doing to me, her tongue finding its way down my stomach.

"Do you want me to do this?" One finger brushed my inner thighs.

"Yes. Please."

:Please.:

Under any circumstances I would have found JT exciting. The sensation of her finger, then fingers, sliding into me was so good I felt orgasm stir. Then I was hit with another wave of pleasure, not from me, but from Her, moaning in tandem with JT's thrusts.

Mari was playing in my head. She was whispering, "Fuck me, Julia."

JT breathed out, "God, you feel good."

:Ooooohhh.:

JT was playing in my head, too. I could see her through my barely open eyes, and what I could see was projected behind my eyes and I knew She could see JT, too. See JT's slick fingers sliding in and out of me, my legs flashing white against JT's black thighs. I knew she could hear my rising wail and my memory of Mari's scream as orgasm tore through her, through me.

JT was crying out. I seized her wrist, pushed her fingers, her hand, as far into me as they would go. I came hard against her palm, harder than I ever remembered and then collapsed, overwhelmed with how good it felt to have her against me and how much more I—we—would need before we were satisfied.

JT was on her back, just breathing. I scrambled between her legs, read the invitation in their spreading beauty.

She tasted like honey and wine, like a woman, and I was drunk on her scent and her heat. I rubbed my forehead and cheeks against the tight, coarse curls of hair and then reveled in the slight sting of her wet against my roughened skin. I noticed sensations, textures, sounds as if I'd never had sex with a woman before, as if it was my first time.

:First time.:

I drank deeply, savored, tried my best to drown in JT's wet. Her legs were around me with crushing force. They jerked as my tongue swirled through her and the images in my head all faded to the midnight blue of concentration. Whatever it took, however long it took. My tongue swirled. JT gasped "Don't stop," and I didn't. Not until she pushed me away.

JT stirred next to me a while later. She kissed my shoulder and then nibbled my ear. "Nice to share a dream with you."

I smiled, but was glad she couldn't see me blushing. For me it had practically been an orgy with memories of Mari mixing with JT in the here and now and the awareness of another presence, watching, enjoying vicariously.

The lights came on. No, not my lights. Lights where She was.

Fear. I felt it ripple through me. I closed my eyes so I could better see what she was looking at.

A face. A man's face. Small brown mustache. Thin lips and scary eyes.

"Your heart rate is way up. Whatever are you dreaming about?"

The beeping sound, so ever present I had tuned it out, was a heart monitor. It was racing.

"I have a feeling I know what. All women are the same."

Through the link between us I sensed his hand on her arm. I felt her agony and exploding anger. These emotions were so familiar to me—he could have been any of a half dozen of my mother's boyfriends. All men are the same, I raged. She was trying to twist away from him.

"You like it."

Another voice: "Ned, what the hell is going on in there?"

Ned answered, "I think she was dreaming or something."

Then he put his head down next to her ear, next to my ear. "You just remember that when Mike is done with you you're mine." His hand squeezed her breast hard—I knew Vina and I would share bruises. "Mine."

The light went out.

I sat bolt upright from the force of molten rage. She was tearing against her bonds, straining with every muscle, but they showed no signs of loosening.

"Save your strength," I said.

JT had sat up, too, one hand to her throat. "I heard him. It was only when I was touching you, but I heard him. Bastard!"

:HELP ME.:

I clutched my head. JT's anger and resolve was a twin to my own. I felt Vina's compassion welling inside me. I knew—I don't know how—that Geri was sobbing, hands over her ears, while Rose was grimly drawing something on a sketch pad.

I saw the four of them, poised, ready, and for some reason irrevocably linked to me. And I was the link to Her.

:HELP ME. PLEASE!:

"Yes," I said. "Whatever it takes, we'll help you."

Chapter 4

roseoday: Geri's right behind me

VINALMOST60: Did anyone else have an unusual night?

MaddyM: !!!!! I don't know about the whole ROAD thing but unless I have a split personality I talked to a woman who is being held prisoner somewhere

roseoday: that's what I woke up with. prisoner, cage, man's face. Geri says she heard a man's voice too

MaddyM: this is JT-still at Julia's. I heard it too, and I wasn't asleep I was right here with Julia when he said he owned this woman.

VINALMOST60: What happened before that? Let's just say it's been a long time, if ever, that I had sex that good. Was I just dreaming? If so, I'd like to go back to sleep!

I squirmed with embarrassment.

MaddyM: it wasn't just you. it was pretty intense.

roseoday: I sketched the face in my dream. I woke

up when he was talking to her. scary. but I'm used to waking up and sketching. I scanned it in and I'll send you the jpeg file. give me a minute

"Want some more coffee?" I nodded, and JT went in the direction of the kitchen. I was having a lot of trouble looking at her. Far as I could tell she wasn't looking at me either.

roseoday: file's on the way

My computer announced that I had mail. I clicked open the message and downloaded the graphic file that Rose had sent. The picture opened after the file saved to my disk. I shuddered.

MaddyM: rose, you're amazing. that's him.
roseoday: takes practice. but my dream images stay with me pretty vividly until I can get them down on paper.

JT looked over my shoulder. "That son-of-a-bitch. He's going to give me more nightmares."
I nodded. "That's him. Exactly as she saw him."

VINALMOST60: Fill me in. My dream was mostly about sex.

I quickly typed out my summary of the "dream," lingering mostly on what happened after the sex. JT added a point or two, then Vina chimed in that her emotional impressions were like mine, including the despair and loneliness of the woman on the other end.

"Why didn't you ask her her name," JT asked after we had all signed off.
"It never really came up. I didn't think I was talking to someone else who needed a name."

53

JT laughed quietly. "I see your point."

Awkward doesn't begin to describe the silence that fell between us.

"I guess I better be heading for home," she finally said. "My shift starts in a few hours."

I mumbled something about e-mailing her if anything happened, then—thankfully—the phone rang. JT let herself out while I sprinted to catch the phone before the answering machine picked up. It was Vina.

"I've been thinking about what to do next," she said, with little preamble.

I was feeling so overwhelmed by the last twenty-four hours that I hadn't gotten that far. "And?"

"Do you think you should work with Shandra again?"

"I don't know. She helped me make contact, but she didn't seem to know what was going on. Maybe."

"Are you open to trying something else?"

I got an uh-oh feeling in the pit of my stomach. "Like what?"

"We can try to find the woman—or we can try to find the man in the picture."

"But how can we find him?" I didn't even know where to start.

"I have a friend who works for the sheriff's department. It seems to me that a brute like that would have a record. His name is Ned. Or Edward. And he has an accomplice named Mike."

"What if he's in Timbuktu? Fresno County Sheriff isn't going to know him."

"Shandra thought they might be close. Because you made contact so quickly."

That made sense, I thought, then I reminded myself that *none* of this made sense. "Maybe it would be worth it."

"You have to come with me, though. My friend will believe what we tell her, but she's a stickler for precision. I never saw the guy's face, but you did."

"When could we meet with her?" I was feeling shaky and

tired.

"This evening, I'm sure. You'll like Gladys. She's a lot like you."

What would a person a lot like me be like? I had no idea. But I agreed to meet her and Gladys at a restaurant around seven that evening.

"Daniel" was the song of the moment when I arrived at the coffee shop on West Shaw. I found Vina and a uniformed sheriff's officer at a booth in the back.

Vina made the introductions. Officer Gladys Nash was in her late forties or early fifties, and she had the very studied blank expression common to police—and IRS auditors, for that matter. It softened slightly whenever she looked at Vina.

"Vina gave me this picture," Gladys said. She pushed it toward me.

I glanced at it and handed it back. "His name is Ned and he's holding a woman captive."

"How exactly do you know that?"

I glanced at Vina, who inclined her head as if to say get on with it.

I stumbled through an explanation of dreams but didn't mention The Road idea, which somehow seemed more flaky than talking to a strange woman in a dream. Silly me.

"Does this woman have a name?"

I had tried to reach her to ask with no luck. Maybe she was sleeping. I knew she wasn't gone because the music was still there. "I didn't ask yet. But I'll find out."

"Do that. I can check missing persons."

"You believe me?"

Gladys Nash didn't answer, but she looked me up and down. No, I was certain, she did not believe me. "Lady V believes you," she said finally. "That's enough for me."

Gladys would do anything for Vina, that was plain. I remembered Shandra's idea that our being lesbians was important.

"How have you been sleeping lately?"

Vina's eyebrows went up with her best don't-be-impertinent warning.

Gladys harrumphed into her coffee. "Santa Anas mean no one gets any sleep, not in my line of work. Considering what I see during the day, no wonder I have nightmares."

"What kind of nightmares?"

"The usual. It would be nice if I could find something to distract me." She glanced for a millisecond in Vina's direction. Vina seemed oblivious.

I opened my mouth to ask for more details, but she picked up her hat.

"Coffee break is over, I'm afraid. When I get off shift later, I'll run this guy's picture through the scanner. I've got a couple of friends in the Tulare and Kern offices who'll do it without asking questions. I'll do a search for Neds with assault records. And the accomplice was Mike, right V?"

Vina nodded. "Thank you, Gladys, for doing this for us."

She wasn't doing it for me, I wanted to say. Gladys said it with a smolder in her eyes that should have melted Vina on the spot. Then Gladys strode away with a truly butch swagger, enhanced by nightstick and gun.

When I glanced back at Vina I caught the flicker of longing in her expression. I puzzled over it while the waitress, who had ignored us until now, took a dinner order from Vina. I decided on a chicken-fried steak. Very comforting, especially with instant mashed potatoes and salty brown gravy.

"How long have you known Gladys?" Considering the way the two felt about each other, I was surprised that they were so distant.

"For years," Vina said. "I met her just after she and my best friend, Suzanne, got together. She and Suzy were madly in love, and Gladys hasn't been the same since Suzy died."

"Oh. How so?"

Vina twisted her napkin. "Oh, she laughed all the time. She

was quite the dancer, too."

"How long ago did Suzy die?"

"Seven years."

I was willing to bet Gladys had spent half those seven years in love with Vina.

"But that's all water under the bridge. I hope she can get us some information."

"Monster Mash" faded away and was replaced by "Smoke on the Water." I felt Her stir, and I closed my eyes.

:Are you there?:

"I'm here." I ignored Vina's startled gasp. "What's your name?"

:Not pronounceable. You can call me whatever you like.:

"Give it to me anyway. So we can help you."

:Difficult. Your language has no sounds for it.:

"Are you Russian or something?"

:No.: I had a fleeting sense of laughter. It rippled through my shoulder blades in a very pleasant fashion.

"We want to try to look you up through the police."

:Police.:

I wasn't surprised when a succession of police officers flitted across my consciousness. Gladys, Jon and Ponch, Lieutenant Tragg, Angie Dickinson, Martin Milner, Broderick Crawford, Andre Brauer. Jimmy Smits looked at a computer printout.

:I will not be in the computer.:

"Oh. That's not going to help us very much."

:Sorry. What's your name?:

"Julia Madison. Some of my friends, well, a few people call me Maddy."

:You can call me whatever you like.:

I opened my eyes. The waitress was standing there with my steak. She looked skeptical about my sanity.

"Thank you," I said sweetly.

When she was out of earshot, I turned to Vina.

"What would a good name for someone from Pallas be? She

57

says her name won't translate."

"Pallas, as in Greece?"

"Not that Pallas, apparently."

"Well," Vina said slowly. "Something from mythology would still be appropriate."

"How about Sirena?" It came to me out of the blue.

Vina said, "Why Sirena?" Her question echoed in my head.

"For Sirens," I said to both of them.

My movie screen filled with a raving Kirk Douglas strapped to the mast of his boat while the Siren song urged him to jump into the sea.

"How appropriate," Vina said.

:I mean you no harm.:

"I know." And I did. "It's still fitting, though."

:Sirena then, if you must.:

With that settled I dug into my mashed potatoes. Vina ate delicately—an omelet with sourdough toast.

"Ask Sirena how she came to be where she is."

:It was an accident.:

I frowned. "Um, Vina, you don't have to ask me to ask, I guess. She can hear you." I was starting to get that creeped-out feeling again. "She says it was an accident."

:I wasn't supposed to be where I was. They found me and brought me here.:

"Where is here?"

:I don't know.:

I finished my steak and nibbled on the well-boiled canned green beans. This is really quite weird, I thought.

:Weird for both of us.:

"Does she know where she is?"

"No," I answered. "And I don't have to talk aloud for her to hear me, either." It's very intrusive, I thought. Next thing you know we'll be doing a repeat of last night.

:Repeat?:

Oh, no you don't, I thought. :Knock it off, Sirena. Sex is off-

58

limits.:

Vina was smiling at me.

"What did I do?"

"I'm laughing at me," Vina said. "I keep forgetting we're not alone."

Marvin Gaye's "Let's Get It On" began to play. :You're doing that on purpose.:

:What on purpose?:

:The music. That song.:

:The music comes from a box.:

I gaped at Vina. "I think I finally thought of something useful to do. Sirena, look at the box."

I closed my eyes to see better through hers, as I had when I'd seen Ned's ugly face. There was a low, corrugated-steel ceiling over her, and as she turned her head I could see cinder-block walls. Where the hell was she?

Her gaze fixed on a small Sony brand radio. On the table next to the radio were numerous objects, but I could only make out gauze and a bottle of rubbing alcohol. I recalled the steady droning beep of the heart monitor. *:Look the other way.:*

Hazily, as if through blurry eyes, I could see a window—high in the wall, just under the roofline. The pane was filled with the orange glow of sunset. The sun was just setting here, too.

The heart monitor looked like I expected one to look—not that I've seen one outside of a television screen. There were various numbers and notes written all over it.

"Is everything okay?"

"Vina, I can see the sunset through her window." I opened my eyes and glanced out the restaurant's window. "That sunset. She's in our time zone, at least." A wave of dizziness hit me and I closed my eyes again.

"Perhaps you should be doing this lying down," Vina said. "Shandra was afraid you'd get overtaxed, remember?"

"I'm glad I ate something."

:Going?:

"I have to for a little while. I'll come back."

:It's getting dark again.:

It was getting easier to respond without talking. *:I will come back. I promise.:*

Vina saw me safely to my car and accepted my protestations that I could drive. I hummed "Me and Mrs. Jones" on the way home, in keeping with Sirena's radio. I had this unusual feeling—hopefulness? As if I was looking forward to an evening of enjoyment. As if I had a date with Sirena or something.

That feeling was the craziest thing to happen so far. That I would actually start to feel good about it—truly bizarre.

:Your English is really improving.:

:Thank you. Or is it just thanks?:

:Thanks is informal, usually between friends or said casually. I'm no English expert, though.:

:Friends? Are we friends?:

Good question, I thought. *:I don't know how I'd describe it. I don't know anything about you, but we've shared some fairly intimate moments.:*

:I am sorry about last night. I opened something private and it was overwhelming. I shouldn't have enjoyed it.:

:That's okay, I guess. That you enjoyed it. I enjoyed it, too. I think JT enjoyed it. Heck, everyone seemed to enjoy it until that creep showed up.:

:Creep?:

I pictured the creepy Ned in my mind.

:Ned. He is evil.:

:What about the guy he called Mike?:

:Mike is a scientist. He is misguided.:

:Is he using you for experiments or something? What kind?:

:He is studying me because I am different.:

:Do me a favor. Look at yourself.:

Two arms, two legs and in between was covered by a white medical drape. In the dark her skin looked pale blue. *:I'm going to* *get you out of there, if I can.:*

:I'm pretty wretched. I haven't been able to get up for several days now.:

:What about...: I didn't have to even think it. She literally read my mind. I told her that the thing she was picturing was called a catheter. The needle in her arm was an IV.

:Tell me everything you've learned about them. It will help us find you.:

:It is very hot here during the day. There's no water outside.:

I remembered her nightmare of searching for water. I was only now beginning to appreciate that everything I'd dreamed had actually happened to her. Falling, running through the desert, finding no water—all magnified through the dream state, but it had still happened to her.

:They don't know that I can translate what they're saying. There was some confusion today about who would see me. They were using a lot of words I didn't follow.:

:Tell me, I'll translate if I know them.:

Password was easy. So was *security*. They also made sense in the context. But most of the rest were gibberish except as single syllables: *comp, way, bars, high, four, shell, toe,* and so on. I could give her ideas about them separately, but they didn't help pinpoint where she was. In the end she learned more than I did.

I was thinking I should probably go to sleep, then I jolted awake thinking about work. Should I go? Couldn't I put the time to better use talking to Sirena?

:You like your work?:

"Yes. I enjoy it because I do it well." I was learning that all I had to do was think about a subject and Sirena absorbed it all. I hardly noticed the movie screens opening and closing.

:I work for my government. I study plants and societies.:

:Sounds interesting.:

:Most of the time. I was not where I was supposed to be, which is how I got here.:

:Are you psychic or something? I mean, have you ever been tested

61

for psychic gifts?:

:*I am sorry. I am not psychic. Not the way you mean it.:*

Not a particularly useful answer. Geri was hearing the music from Sirena's radio. Rose saw and remembered pictures while she slept. JT was getting part of the sight and sound of my experience with Sirena, and Vina was getting all the emotion and sensation.

:*I am sorry. For all of you. If I knew another way. If I thought this would hurt you. If...:*

I felt Sirena's longing and pain as if it were my own. In some ways it was. "It's okay. We can help you. We will."

On an impulse I got off the bed and staggered to the computer. Shandra was right about one thing—communicating with Sirena was draining. I scrabbled a bag of M&M's out of my desk as my computer booted up. Tomorrow I'd have to go shopping and replenish my supply of Hostess Cupcakes and powdered cake donuts.

I sent a message to Geri telling her that the music was from a radio. Not a CD player or cassette, but a radio, which meant a radio station. I would search up and down the dial for a match and asked her to do the same. I sent a second message to the whole group about the meeting with Gladys Nash and the fact that Sirena and I saw the sunset at roughly the same time. And I explained how Sirena got her name.

Just after I sent the second message my screen beeped with an invitation to chat.

roseoday: **Geri's trying to sleep, but if she wakes I'll tell her about the radio**

MaddyM: thanks. I have a favor to ask you

roseoday: **fire away**

MaddyM: could you scan and send me your sketches from the last two weeks? I'm wondering if they'll match my dreams and if I show them to Sirena she might remember something useful.

roseoday: **sure. It'll take me 15 mins or so**

MaddyM: fine. She was in the desert and we have lots of desert around here.

roseoday: **Mojave, maybe? I had lots of desert images. And snowy mountains.**

MaddyM: yeah, that's a match for me.

Sirena was getting drowsy. I could tell because I was, too.

:Sleep. I think there is a drug in the IV. I don't normally sleep so much.:

The lights came on where she was, and her eyes fluttered open. It wasn't Ned but a new face. He was balding and pasty white as if he hadn't been in the sun for years. His lips were thin and turned down with a lifetime of disappointment. Suspicion and cruelty filled his lifeless brown eyes.

MaddyM: Rose! Can you go to sleep right now?

roseoday: **yeah right**

MaddyM: it's a new face. There's a different guy with Sirena.

roseoday: **I take about 45 mins to fall asleep and that's only after midnight or so. wish i could drop off right now. Like I said, if I could do what I do while awake I'd be rich.**

Mike leaned over Sirena, and I felt the prick in her arm. "Your blood won't type," he whined, as if it were her fault.

:Tough shit.:

I was teaching Sirena bad words.

MaddyM: We'll get a chance. You could act as my sketch artist, maybe.

roseoday: **I'm not so good at that, but we could try. your jpegs are on the way.**

MaddyM: thanks. I'll download and send messages to everybody if Sirena remembers

something.
    roseoday: **good.**

Mike was still muttering at Sirena as he drew more blood, then clipped a fingernail and a lock of hair. Animal, I growled in my mind.

I sent the scanned jpegs to print on my color inkjet. I'd study them over my morning coffee when I was more alert. When they were done printing I shut down and went back to bed.

:Is he almost done?:

:I hope so. He keeps taking samples from me as if they will tell him something.:

I could see Mike through her eyes, frowning and babbling. He straightened from prodding at her knee joint and said with a resigned sigh, "I didn't want to have to do this."

I shuddered when he pulled the drape over her middle down. Unlike Ned, his manner was impersonal, but the humiliation was the same. I flushed with anger.

:It's okay.:

:You don't need to comfort me. I know how you feel, that's all.:

Sirena did whatever she did to make my movie screens come on. I didn't want them to but she followed the links in my head with ease. Just as the first ugly image from my youth appeared, a bolt of pain shocked through Sirena and then through me.

I screeched. It was so unexpected and so awfully painful. I clutched my ribs just under my left breast. When I looked at my hands I was surprised they weren't bloody.

Sirena made no sound though her whole body shook.

"You do feel pain, then." Mike nodded as if making a scientific note to himself. A bloodied scalpel dangled from his fingertips.

It was then that I told myself I'd find that fucking Mengele and somehow I'd make him pay.

"But why don't you speak? Are you mute? Do you have vocal chords?"

The scalpel dipped toward Sirena again and he made another

light incision, this time under her other breast.

I bit back my scream. My phone began to ring. I heard Vina on the answering machine demanding to know what in heaven's name was going on.

Sirena's smoldering anger blossomed, and I wanted to tear the house down. *:You can make me understand your pain, why not him? Sirena, make him stop.:*

:I can't! I can't talk. My hands are tied, I can't write, I can't think at him like with you—he's blank.:

He kept cutting, the fool. He was trying to make Sirena cry out when she couldn't talk, and all he had to do was untie her hands. The pain was more manageable until Mike held up a thin piece of flesh about the size of a quarter.

I don't know how I kept my dinner down. He put his bloody sample on a large slide, muttering about DNA, then put gauze on the wound he'd made and sprayed it with something. The pain diminished to almost nothing. Bastard. He'd had local anesthesia all along.

The phone rang again, and I heard JT's voice. I managed to pick up the receiver.

"Maddy, what the fuck was that? I was sound asleep, and Jesus Christ I thought my skin was peeling off."

I swallowed hard. "He...he, the other guy. Mike. He took a skin sample from her."

"Jesus fucking H. Christ. Is she okay?"

:I am okay.:

She wasn't. I could tell.

"She's pretty shaky and trying to hide it. The guy is picking her apart. And she's mute, JT. Even though she's learning English very fast she can't talk. Her hands are tied."

"This is a nightmare, a fucking nightmare. How are we going to find this bastard?"

"I don't know. We all have to try, though."

"Why us? Why is this happening to us?"

I wish I knew, I told her, then I asked her to call Rose and Geri while I called Vina.

"I just got off the phone with Gladys," Vina said with her usual lack of preambles. "I was quite frightened, and I thought I might ask her to check on you."

"I'm okay, for now. How much of what happened did you feel?"

Vina was silent for a moment. "I'm not bleeding, but Bactine is not going to take the sting out of these...scars. Do you want to know something interesting?"

"You mean more interesting than all of this?" I could hardly imagine what it might be.

"It's on topic," Vina said firmly. "Gladys was awake when I called her. She confessed to having just woken from a nightmare and could only say it was about a bogeyman with a knife. He had a knife, right?"

"A scalpel—close enough. Yes, and you're right, that is very interesting. I think tomorrow I'll talk to some of my lesbian friends and see if they had a nightmare."

"If they did, what does that tell us?"

"I have no idea. But information is what we need, or I swear he's going to kill her. He's worse than the other one because he doesn't even see her as a person to use. She's an object to him."

Vina assured me she would also call her lesbian friends. Who knew what it would get us, but anything we gained would be worth the effort.

The light went out in Sirena's room, and she closed her eyes. I felt hot tears trickle down her temples and into her ears. I hate that.

There was no one to hold her, or tell her everything would be okay except me. :*I'm still here. We'll help, I promise. Please sleep if you can.*:

:*I don't have a choice.*: With her heart rate slowing, I could tell Sirena was getting drowsy again.

:*We'll help. I promise.*: What else could I say? I remembered all those times I would have given anything for my mother to hold

66

me and promise I'd be okay, promise it wouldn't happen again.

:I believe you. You said you knew how I felt. Maybe that is why I can think to you.:

:Have you thought to other people?:

She was silent for a long time. I almost thought she had fallen asleep.

:I don't want to scare you away again.:

:I don't think you can.:

:I have thought to other people. My sisters, my mother.:

:Hmm. It sort of makes sense within a family. But Strange Universe would be interested in your story.:

Her laugh trailed away into a sigh. *:More than you know.:*

:Or could possibly understand, I'll bet.:

:You have a vast capacity for understanding.: I could tell she was fighting off sleep. *:That's probably why I am communicating with you so clearly.:*

The image of the first of my mother's boyfriends to assault me unfolded inside my head. I cringed. *:Don't—:*

:I'm not...:

She wasn't. Or maybe she was and didn't realize it. It was like what I was calling "The Mari Sex Movie" JT and I had shared. Since she left I didn't want to think about how good sex with her had been, mostly because I wasn't likely to have anything so good in the near future. It's kind of like trying not to think about chocolate when you're dieting. But Sirena had touched briefly on one image with Mari and the whole movie had played.

This was the same. There he was, Jack Daniels, ha ha, his favorite drink, too. I had been twelve and I'd just gotten my first period. I guess my mother told him because he said I was only halfway to being a woman and he'd help me the rest of the way.

:Forget...:

:I can't.:

:Forget...:

The image began to fade. Sirena was literally pushing it away. Her effort was more than my mother had ever managed. It had taken nearly three years of therapy before I stopped reliving the assaults when an associated sound or smell triggered it, like the smell of liquor.

Sirena continued to smooth the image away. It went all gray, and then another image unfolded, of a much happier time, my first year in college. She'd chosen well. She saw the campus at Cal through my eyes, the Campanile, the Bear's Lair, heard the plastic drum musicians, smelled the falafel.

I floated on the pleasantness of those days. When Janice, my very-first-ever woman lover, slipped into the movie, I wasn't embarrassed. I felt Sirena drifting off to sleep as I relived the panic-filled but oh-so-joyous moments in Janice's dorm room. Her fingers slipped between my legs, our tongues tangled in rising need.

A deep sigh of release rolled over me, and I joined Sirena in exhausted sleep.

Chapter 5

I woke up Monday morning refreshed by uninterrupted, deep sleep. I felt whole. Sirena was silent, and Chicago's "Feelin' Stronger Every Day" was almost pleasant as background music in my head.

I studied Rose's pictures over coffee, oatmeal and cinnamon toast. They were strikingly like the images in my "nightmares"— a menacing black machine against an orange sunset, white mountains. The earliest was of checkerboard farmland, as if from an airplane. It stirred that first nightmare back to memory, that of falling. Could Sirena have been in a parachuting accident? I mentally prodded the place in my head where Sirena's voice seemed to originate, but she didn't respond.

I called JT, who had left me her number at the hospital if I needed it. She answered brusquely.

"I need a favor, and maybe you can help."

"I'll be happy to check into that," she said.

Hmm. "Is someone listening?"

"That's correct."

"Oh. Well. What I need is a doctor's excuse. I want to take time off and I can't use vacation time—I have a ton—unless it's prescheduled. So a temporary illness is what I need."

"I can help you with that if you can give me an idea of symptoms."

"Well, I went to the doctor a week ago for migraine, nausea, fever and unexplained pain. That's when I got the sleeping pills."

"That treatment is usually lengthy. A week, I believe?"

"A week sounds good." A week was actually perfect. Emily would go through my in-box and reassign stuff that needed prompt attention, and my work completion log was already available to her on the main server. I was glad I'd put in extra time on Friday getting everything shipshape.

"I'll be able to do that right away, doctor." I snickered, and JT became more brusque. "Is there something else I can do for you?"

"Sorry, I'll never make a spy 'cause I get the giggles. You want to fax whatever it is to me?"

"That number is on file, isn't it?"

"Um—yeah, fax it to my home number, that's what you mean, right?"

"That's correct."

"Thank you, JT. I think we have to move fast, but I don't really want to lose my job."

"That's a logical conclusion," JT said. "Thank you for calling, doctor."

I snickered again as I hung up.

:What is a spy?:

I was getting used to her—I wasn't startled by Sirena's sudden return. *:Someone who pretends to be someone else I guess. To get information they wouldn't otherwise have access to.:*

:Oh.:

I set up my computer to receive and print a fax, then spread Rose's sketches out on the table. *:Do any of these images look familiar to you?:*

:Yes. The figures, the mountains, yes.:

70

:Did you fall out of an airplane?: I indicated the sketch of farmland.

Sirena hesitated. *:No. I don't...remember.:*

:Yes, you do.: I was certain of it. I had a flash of inspiration.: *You're a spy, aren't you? I mean, you're in this country illegally, and you didn't mean to get caught. So your own government isn't looking for you. They would disavow all knowledge of your actions.:* Sirena shared my mental image of a tape self-destructing.

:I am an observer. I told you the truth. I study plants and societies for the simple acquisition of knowledge. But you are right, my government will not come looking for me. We never anticipated I would end up in this situation.:

I thought she was telling the truth, but I had a niggling doubt I couldn't pin down.

The phone rang, and I heard my computer connecting to someone's fax machine. A few minutes later a very official looking doctor's treatment statement flopped out of the printer. Wow. I had a severe case of salmonella poisoning and anemia and would not be able to report to work for seven days. Cool.

Aware that Sirena was observing everything I did, but somehow not minding it, I called Emily and lied about being ill and said I'd fax her my doctor's statement. Then I called Carol and told her I wasn't that sick and assured her she needn't worry.

"I'm having nightmares, that's all."

"Nightmares? That's bizarre." Carol's tone said she never had nightmares, which answered my next question. "What kind of nightmares?"

"Oh, I think they're related to some stuff that happened to me a long time ago. I thought I'd put it behind me, but maybe not." I twisted the phone cord around my finger and thought about how lies can come back to bite you. I'd stopped lying to myself, for the most part, but I was lying to everyone else.

"So you're going to, like, have some intense therapy or something?"

"Something like that." I was willing to bet the next week

would be intense. "I didn't want it to get around the office, so Emily thinks I have food poisoning."

"Well, if you need anything I'm here."

"Thanks for the offer," I said, touched. "I'll be fine."

She believed me, why wouldn't she? "Toodles, then."

I hung up with the oddest feeling I might not see Carol again. What's that expression? Someone walking over my grave?

:You are not used to people offering to help you, are you?:

"That's an understatement." I felt the pin-sifting sensation suddenly start up. "And if I wanted you to know more about me, I'd share it," I said tartly.

:Sorry. Just curious. I have never met anyone like you.:

"Ditto."

She searched my brain for a definition of ditto, but I could tell that was all she was doing. I was getting used to the different pressures of her searches and was beginning to be able to tell exactly what Sirena was up to. Perhaps that's why I was so at peace this morning. I no longer felt out of control.

I called a dozen of the lesbians in my address book and asked them all about nightmares under the pretext of helping a friend with her doctoral dissertation. Most were forthcoming with answers, though I could tell those that had been Mari's friends thought I was as strange as always.

I munched on a Pop Tart and looked at my results.

:What are you trying to deduce?:

Her English was getting quite good, I thought. *:Well, I want to find out if you're just disturbing only lesbians or not. It's hard to tell.:*

:Lesbians?:

I let her search freely for definitions. I wasn't going to put it into words. I closed my eyes and let Sirena sift through images of every lesbian I'd ever known, every gathering, picnic, pride parade, festival and meeting. I wanted her to understand I was talking about more than just a sex act, because I had no idea how homosexuals were viewed where she was from.

The movie screens overflowed with my experience of the

gay community in Fresno. Small, at times frightened, but always proud. I guided Sirena from my own memories to books I'd read and movies I'd seen. The last image before she stopped was from *Priscilla, Queen of the Desert.*

:I understand, I think. You have more options than where I come from.:

This I could believe, especially since she'd seen my last trip up to San Francisco for the pride parade. Nowhere else was quite as option-open as San Francisco.

I cringed as "Dueling Banjos" started on Sirena's radio. "It would be so great if they would shut that off."

:I've learned a lot from the music. Not just the words, but the musical language. It is sophisticated.:

Sophisticated? I like pop music as much as the next person, but that wasn't the adjective I'd use to describe it. I put on a Bach CD. *:This is sophisticated music.:*

Sirena listened to the music, and her gratitude to have a distraction from her circumstances was sincere. I hummed along from time to time.

I don't know quite why, but I suddenly had what I can only call a reality check. I was sitting on the sofa when I should have been at work, listening to Bach and trying to explain to a voice *in my head* why it was sophisticated, and I believed that voice belonged to a woman from another country being held captive by some goons in the desert.

Hello! Earth to Maddy! I could almost hear my mother saying it.

What on earth was I doing?

:Helping me. Just being there, distracting me. You have no idea how much this helps. I was going mad.:

I reminded myself it wasn't just me. That Rose and I saw the same things, Vina and I felt them, JT and I dreamed them, and Gina and I heard them. We were all lesbians, and at least three of my lesbian friends confessed to an increase in nightmares lately. One had even mentioned dreaming about being operated on without anesthesia. They all put it down to the Santa Anas.

I needed to think, and I needed some lunch. A jog past Ernie's Rib Hut would help with both. I was pulling an almost clean T-shirt over my head when Sirena got excited.

:*I know this music! I've heard it before.*:

"Finally! Something we have in common." I knew the piece by heart of course, the Prelude from the *Well Tempered Clavier*, Bach's masterwork of both counterpoint and mathematics posing as a simple piano exercise. I loved it, especially this version performed by Glenn Gould.

:*What does it mean?*:

I snapped back to alertness. :*Mean?*:

:*What is it saying?*:

I love music, but I never majored in it. "Its meaning isn't a literal one. It's art. It's expression of creativity. It's...it's just beautiful."

Sirena seemed dumbfounded. I could tell a million questions bubbled in her, but she held them back for several minutes. She rustled around in my head a little, looking for something. My mental movie screen flashed with all I knew about musical notation, keys, sharps and flats, which wasn't much.

Then Sirena began to laugh. I felt it tickle in my nerves and blood. I smiled. Her joy was infectious. It was as if I had answered some great question for her and she was pleased beyond description by my answer.

"What's so funny?" I was willing to bet that Vina had a great big smile on her face.

:*It's hard to explain. I didn't understand music until now.*:

:*Oh. Well, glad I could oblige.*:

:*Thank you. If I ever get home I'll have a lot to talk about.*:

The door to the room where Sirena was kept banged open and she jumped. My heart went up in to my throat.

Mike checked the incisions he'd made, grunted, then stepped back out of Sirena's sight. Someone else stepped forward.

It was a woman, not as tall as Mike. Her eyes were not as evil as Ned's nor as crazy as Mike's. But they were obsessive, and her gaze flitted around the room, not missing a detail.

"Has she said anything? Tried to make any contact?"

Mike grunted.

"I have to know this is for real," the woman said. Her voice was thin and nasal. There was a slight drawl, midwestern, perhaps.

Through the link I could feel Sirena's hand being lifted, but I couldn't see it.

The woman whistled. "Okay, I might believe this. But it could still just be clever surgery and a little bad tanning problem."

:Sirena, what are they talking about?:

:I told you I was different, and Mike is trying to quantify exactly how.:

"I'm not going to pop for a portable X-ray machine," the woman was saying. "Not until I get a signed contract for an exclusive."

A reporter? This woman was a reporter? What kind of filth let another women be used for experimentation and then bartered on the rights to her story?

"Whatever," Mike said. "I just need that machine. I'm sure it'll turn up something."

The woman leaned over Sirena and peered into her eyes. "Why don't you talk? I can tell you're following all of this." She frowned. "You're feeding her, right?"

Mike tapped the IV bag.

"Oh come on," the woman snapped. "How about real food? And moving around? She's going to get bedsores if she doesn't have them by now."

"We gave her some food, and she was sick everywhere. Better to stick with basic nutrients. And she has to stay confined. She's very strong. And she moves fast. We haven't found the wreck yet, but we're already out to a fifty-mile radius."

A plane wreck? Hard to believe that our own searchers weren't out there. Edwards Air Force Base—and the desert where I believed Sirena must be—was to our south, and air traffic in the entire desert area was monitored by radar.

"Maybe she destroyed it."

"Maybe." Mike put his hand on the woman's arm, as if to draw her away from Sirena.

She glared at his hand until he removed it, then turned back to Sirena. She looked down into Sirena's eyes with a piercing depth that made me feel as if she could see through Sirena all the way to me. "Who are you? Where are you from?"

Mike was fiddling with Sirena's IV, and I felt Sirena get woozy. "I want her to sleep," he muttered. "Let's go back to the big room."

The woman gave him a peeved look. "By all means. Just remember she's not a laboratory animal."

Mike's smile was ugly. "Maybe she is, Tamar."

"That's Ms. Reese, to you."

Sirena was out, and I relived the conversation, picking it over for clues. If only I had made notes. I cursed myself mentally—my computer was on, I could have typed it, at least the key parts.

But I did remember the important things. Sirena was being held in a compound. Something about her was press worthy. And a reporter named Tamar Reese knew where Sirena was.

My run was forgotten. I microwaved a Hot Pocket, then sat down at my computer to write messages.

VINALMOST60: It has to be a pseudonym. I've looked in all the resources I can think of. No journalist or author under Tamar Reese or Rhys or Rees or any other variation I tried.

roseoday: Geri here. should I wake Rose up?

MaddyM: No! Mike is fussing around her. Maybe Rose will get his face.

VINALMOST60: I hope he doesn't touch her

MaddyM: me too

JTbabe: what do we do now?

VINALMOST60: I'll keep looking. I'll try the journalist associations, too.

JTbabe: this smacks of National Weekly Star or The Enquirer or something. I mean who else would print a story about a woman being tortured?

MaddyM: I guess if I wrote for one of those — wait.

Mike was looking in Sirena's eyes with a thin-beamed penlight. Then he looked in her ears.

"Well?" I recognized Tamar's voice, and willed her to move so Sirena could see her—so Rose could see and sketch her, too.

"Well, what?" Mike pulled Sirena's lip down to look at her teeth.

"Are you going to sign the contract or do I leave?"

"You leave when I say so."

Tamar moved into view. Mike's back was to her, but she was in full view of Sirena. Her mouth was downturned with loathing as she looked at Mike's back. She glanced at Sirena and her entire face changed—obsession, yes, but for the first time, compassion. Sirena saw it, too, because I felt her hope resonate in me.

MaddyM: Rose might get Tamar, too. If we could find Tamar she might help us—she's at least sympathetic to how Sirena is being treated

VINALMOST60: Sirena is relieved.

MaddyM: yeah

roseoday: Rose is waking up, she's grabbed her sketchpad.

MaddyM: yayayayayay!

roseoday: listen. Funny Face, the Donna Fargo version I think.

MaddyM: is that what that song is. never heard it before.

JTbabe: it's from 71? 70?

roseoday: 73 I think everything is from that year or earlier

MaddyM: don't try to tell me she's stuck in a different time or something. I don't do time paradoxes. Saw enough on star trek. past is future. future is past, makes me dizzy.

roseoday: **LOL. Well, I've been listening on the dial and can't match the radio station. It's all oldies, though. Vina, how would I look up the station call numbers for this area?**

VINALMOST60: I'm laughing too. Where most people forget to look—try the yellow pages, dear. You can also find them online through FCC.gov.

Mike and Tamar left Sirena's room. The overhead light went out, leaving only a wan reddish glow from the high windows. I felt Sirena's rush of despair—another day ending in captivity.

roseoday: **Rose wants the keyboard. I think I'll skeedaddle to the yellow pages. I'll call stations tomorrow and ask what song they're playing until I get a match. I'll probably get nowhere fast.**

I looked out at the darkening sky. It was brilliant red—all the dust from the winds adding to the expected orange of smog.

MaddyM: we've lost another day somehow and I don't feel like we're getting anywhere

JTbabe: hang in there, Julia. I wish there was more I could do. I'm just not as affected as the rest of you except when I'm near Julia.

roseoday: **Geri's gone to get me some coffee. She's a good woman. I'm scanning the sketches. Man and woman. You'll have them in a few minutes.**

MaddyM: JT, why do you suppose you're not getting impressions as vividly as the rest of us?

JTbabe: hell if I know.

VINALMOST60: Julia, did you get a chance to make those phone calls?

MaddyM: yes. but I don't know what it told me. I called 12 friends, well, sort of friends. 3 said they were having bizarre nightmares and all 3 blamed them on the Santa Anas. The other 9 said they weren't having nightmares. I don't think this will get us anywhere. there must be another common factor.

JTbabe: if we knew the common factor what would that get us

roseoday: **allies.**

The word put a chill down my spine. Allies made me think of war, and I was not cut out to be a soldier.

JTbabe: you're scaring me rose

roseoday: **I suppose this wouldn't be a good time to say my daddy was IRA, would it? and I did a bit of organizing in my student days**

MaddyM: now I'm scared. I hadn't thought about—where this might lead. what we're going to have to do to free her. she's in a compound, which means security.

Several minutes passed, then Rose's sketches arrived. I busied myself with opening and printing them—they were as accurate as her earlier work. I did not want to think about masterminding some sort of jailbreak. And going to the authorities was out of the question. Gladys was only helping because she was in love with Vina. Then I had a chilling thought.

MaddyM: How do we know Mike isn't CIA or something? Since Sirena is a foreigner?

JTbabe: why would CIA have a reporter there?

I was slightly reassured.

:Please tell them that I've heard nothing to make me think Mike or Ned are government people. They don't talk about rules or goals or

having superiors to report to.:

I laughed to myself. Sirena knew her bureaucratic tendencies.

MaddyM: Sirena doesn't think they're official-type people. Rose, your sketches are right on.

JTbabe: Tamar's kinda cute.

MaddyM: you didn't see her eyes. She's a woman with an obsession. the more I think about it, the more I think she's lying to Mike about something.

VINALMOST60: There is something sinister at play here.

roseoday: I find it hard to believe that our all being lesbian is a coincidence

JTbabe: maybe we all eat tofu and wear birkenstocks, too. that could be a common factor.

MaddyM: maybe I should see Shandra again

roseoday: I don't think it could hurt

VINALMOST60: Hang on, i'm getting a message from Gladys

:Julia, please thank everyone. I can't believe that help is coming. That I was able to communicate with you. I think you are all remarkable.:
I passed on Sirena's thoughts, then Vina was back.

VINALMOST60: Gladys says she might have a line on our Ned. Nothing for a Mike though. I told her I could get her a sketch of Mike and another accomplice in the morning. A Ned Sandusky fitting this description served 6 months for sexual battery of his girlfriend.

JTbabe: don't you love that euphemism, sexual battery?

MaddyM: that could be Ned. he's a predator. he's raped before and maybe worse.

80

VINALMOST60: Gladys doesn't have any way of knowing where he is. He's broken his parole and there is a warrant out for him.

Damn. All we were getting was more information that didn't lead us any closer to Sirena. Where was she? How could we close in on her location?

MaddyM: I'll think about seeing Shandra tomorrow. Don't know.
roseoday: Geri says don't be discouraged
VINALMOST60: Easier said than done. Good night all.

I sat staring at my screen long after the chat window had emptied. I felt as if I was walking in quicksand. Even as I thought it, I felt Sirena looking up quicksand in whatever substituted as a dictionary in my head.

:*At least you and I can communicate more easily than before. I am not making you nuts.*:

I laughed ruefully. :*Not nuts, but something equally dangerous. I believe this is really happening instead of being insane. I'm not sure that's a good thing.*:

:*Am I putting you in danger:*?

:*Maybe.*: I had to be honest. I was scared. It never occurred to me that I had any choice but to act.

:*No, I cannot allow this.*:

I felt a definite clicking sensation. The radio remained ("Playground in My Mind"), but Sirena was gone. I thought as loudly as possible. :*After all this you're wrong if you think YOU get to decide what happens to ME. I AM GOING TO HELP YOU, LIKE IT OR NOT!*:

Nothing.

:*SIRENA!*:

:*Stop yelling at me.*:

I propped my chin on one hand and stared at the empty screen.

:You should stop fooling yourself that this is all one way anymore.:

:You've learned a lot.:

:I don't feel like it. I don't feel any different than I did before. This ability, or whatever it is, is all coming from you.:

Sirena's chuckle was warm. *:Now who is fooling herself?:*

I was a pro at lying to myself. Funny, I thought. Ever since I'd accepted that Sirena existed I hadn't been telling myself lots of lies to get through the day.

Something was going right in my life, in a bassackward sort of way.

In honor of feeling pretty good I had pizza delivered. Sirena seemed to vicariously enjoy the meatlike sausage and pepperoni, the pseudocheese melted gooey orange stuff on top, not to mention what passed for sauce with a tomato base. I love cheap pizza. An Island Punch Snapple topped off the meal.

I fell asleep in front of the TV. Not surprising. It felt so good to be asleep.

Uh-oh. I was asleep and knew I was asleep. Which meant part of me wasn't asleep.

Sirena was likewise sleep-awake. *:Julia, you should be resting.:*

:Yes, mother.: It was an unfortunate choice of words, because I was asleep. I began to dream about my mother.

At this time of night she would be playing blackjack herself, or acting as "luck" for someone who was. She'd told me once, not that I had wanted to know, that menopause had given her more nights not spent at home. She had said it with her cigarette-bourbon laugh, half-wheezing and louder than the joke warranted. Not that I thought it was a laughing matter. She was lucky she hadn't caught something terminal. For all I knew she had.

:She bore you, yet you do not respect or love her.:

:I got over loving her a long time ago.:

:That is sad.:

Sad, but necessary. I'd been an inconvenience, then a useful housemaid, and, when I got older and her boyfriends started to take notice of me, I became competition to be denigrated. After the first assault I'd taken to wearing big clothes. I'd gained weight and done my best to make myself unattractive. Jack Daniels left. They all left. But now, instead of saying my clinging and whining had driven them away, it was my sullen ugliness that cost us our latest meal ticket. And so it went for all the years until I left for college, and left living in a trailer park forever. There was nothing to love there. There had never been any love there.

:Why was she permitted to have children?:

:Permitted by whom? It's her body.:

:Where are her friends? Her family, her circle?:

:There were none, none and none.: Just the boyfriends.:

:That is sad, also.:

It was. But I was drifting into deeper sleep at last.

My last conscious thought was that Sirena's touch in my mind was gentle and soothing. It was everything my mother's touch had never been.

:Thank you.:

:Go to sleep, Maddy.:

I tumbled deeper and felt Sirena drift away. Mari visited me—she was so warm, so tender. I floated in her arms while ivory-colored fronds brushed toward a coral sky. Mari made love to me, and then she rocked me to even deeper sleep.

Chapter 6

Finding Tamar became my goal. If we found her, we would find Sirena. Tamar might not be an ally, but she wasn't Mike's ally either. What I needed was someone good at finding things who wouldn't ask any questions. I considered calling Shandra, but the prospect didn't fill me with hope. While she'd been right that I had some sort of link to Sirena, she hadn't seemed to know how to hone in on it.

Instead, I decided to do something I knew I'd regret, but what else was new? I wanted to get to Sirena, and it really didn't matter what stones I turned over in the search. Like JT had said, at some point dignity had fallen in my priorities.

I called Jaja Jajou, a friend of Mari's. Jaja was a fortune-teller, which I thought was all hokum. Had thought. Well, still thought. But once at a party I'd seen her tell the host where to find her car keys. At the time I thought it was a put-up job, but Mari had been convinced and had consulted Jaja a couple of times for advice. First trip was about her job. Second about her family. Third was about me, and the last trip I knew about was how soon she should leave me for Fran.

Well, isn't this special, I thought as I dialed Jaja's number. I've been to an adept, and now I was going to a clairvoyant. What next, water divination? Walking on red-hot coals? Running with the wolves? 1-900-PSYCHIC?

Jaja was happy to hear from me. She'd known I was going to call, wasn't that amazing? Simply amazing, I agreed, and we set an after-lunch appointment.

:*Maddy, what is an X-ray machine?*:

:*Good morning to you, too.*: I sat down at the table with a fresh cup of coffee, extra cream, and a Pop Tart.

:*Good morning.*:

I don't really know how an X-ray machine works, but I guess I knew enough for Sirena to get the picture.

:*He cannot use one on me.*:

:*I agree, but even if we don't get there before he does, it's only a few exposures.*:

:*He can't use one on me. I'm different.*:

"You keep saying that. How are you different?" I bit into the Pop Tart and burned my tongue on the strawberry filling. I hate that.

:*I...am put together differently.*:

:*We're all different. Look, you're female, right?*:

Her yes was hesitant. :*I am still different from you. The X-ray might kill me*:

That seemed a little far-fetched. I mean, kill her? :*Sirena, I don't see—*:

:*You don't believe me, but I feel it. Maddy, I'm going to die here in this place. Strapped to this table!*:

Desperation and despair welled across the link between us, and I fought to stay calm. :*You've been confined for a week now, right? You're not thinking clearly.*:

:*Go fuck yourself.*:

Wow. Sirena had really picked up my language. :*I know you don't mean that—*:

:*Don't pat-patronize me! I understand my circumstances and you don't! Once he sees my insides he's going to cut me open and probably not care if I'm dead first. If I'm going to die, at least let me do it my own way! We have a ritual—:*

My wrists ached as she futilely pulled against her bonds. *:Calm down! You're not mad at me!:* I clutched my head and thought hard about an empty beach with soft surf and a light breeze.

:Son-of-a-bitch! Zzick! I'm not a robot. I'm not an animal.:

Palm trees swaying in the wind. The cheeping of a tern. A rich blue sky.

:I can't believe this is happening to me. I don't deserve this. What did I do to deserve this?: Her hysteria seemed to ease, but she had found a refrain I had known long ago.

:No one deserves to be a victim. You didn't do anything wrong.: I laughed humorlessly. When the first therapist told me that I had told her to go fuck herself.

Sirena was crying quietly, her eyes shut tight. From far away, through her ears, I heard voices.

"If she dies there's no money, no publicity, no nothing." That was Tamar's voice. She sounded plenty pissed.

Mike was mumbling, and Sirena could have cared less about what he was saying anyway. I picked up, "...increasing sedative."

"You know what happens to creatures kept in captivity who aren't used to it? They go crazy, Mike. Some animals in zoos pace back and forth endlessly, the rest of their mind completely gone. By the time you figure her out she could be crazy as a loon if you don't give her some freedom."

:I am not a bear. I am not a loon.: Sirena seemed very distant.

I put my head down on the table, suddenly weary. *:If you don't keep your head we're all going to be loony.:*

Incredibly, I felt her giggle. She'd turned on my movie screens and found all the Monty Python references to loonies and looniness.

:If you can find Monty Python funny there's hope for you.:

I felt Sirena's conscious effort to keep from hysterical laughter. *:What's funny is you think they're funny.:*

:They are!: Well, she'd impugned Monty Python. She was as

bad as Mari.

:*Hmmm...Mari.*: The movie screens flickered and there she was on the kitchen floor the day we moved into the house. Some people put in shelf paper. Mari wanted to have sex in every room.

:*Stop that! Really, that's private.*:

The movie screens turned off. :*Sorry. Just looking to divert myself.*:

Mike's voice intruded. "See, her heart rate is back to normal. She's fine."

"As if you're a doctor." Tamar's voice came through loud and clear.

"I am."

"A doctor of what? Electronics? If you're a medical doctor I want to see a diploma."

"I've studied medicine extensively," Mike said haughtily.

"Sure, and that's why you're in the middle of goddamn nowhere surrounded by satellite dishes and radio antennas, eating out of cans with that sick-o Ned for company."

"Ned has his uses," Mike said, his tone turning smug.

"He lays a hand on me again I'll kick him so hard his whole family will feel it." I hoped Ned did get out of line—I had no doubt that Tamar could do what she threatened. "This is all crap," she snapped.

Sirena opened her eyes slightly. Tamar was backing Mike up against a table. Lightning was practically crackling in her eyes.

:*She's strong.*:

:*Strong and loony.*: I felt Sirena smile.

"I've had it with your cloak-and-dagger shit," Tamar said through gritted teeth. "This is all a fake, and you can take me back to town, you sick fuck. And if you try putting a blindfold on me again I'll rip your fucking arm out of the socket."

"A fake? You think this is a fake?" Mike shoved Tamar to one side.

I'll never forget Tamar's look of horror as Mike advanced on

Sirena. Sirena tried to throw herself off the table, with as much success as the last hundred times she'd tried it.

He had the scalpel.

Tamar screamed, "No." She snatched up a stool and advanced on Mike, but she was too late.

I fell to the floor, writhing in pain. My left hand spasmed uncontrollably, and before my eyes a huge, blood-filled bruise swelled.

Sirena was convulsing in agony.

"Look at that," Mike screamed. He grabbed Tamar by the arm and dragged her forward. Tamar looked as if she was going to throw up.

Then her face changed. "Holy Mother of God."

"That's got nothing to do with God."

:Helpme helpme helpme helpme helpme helpme helpme helpme...:

Sirena's ululating cry went on and on. I could no longer hear Mike or Tamar, but at some point somebody did something for her hand and the pain diminished slightly. But her cry remained.

Through it all, "It Never Rains in Southern California" played on the radio.

I was late to my appointment with Jaja.

Sirena had fallen into exhausted sleep, helped along by something in her IV. I managed to pull myself together enough to put ice on my hand and eat a second breakfast—the entire scene had left me feeling completely empty and shaky.

Vina had called while I scarfed down my third toaster waffle. She was as near hysterical as she could be. She'd left work claiming a stack of books had fallen on her hand. I'd managed to tell her what was happening to Sirena, but some of it was too awful to say aloud. I didn't have to be explicit—Vina understood. She said she would take Rose's sketches of Mike and Tamar to Gladys as soon as she stopped shaking.

Geri had called shortly after Vina. She reported that she'd called every radio station in the book with no matches for the music she heard. Then she'd asked if I was okay, because for a few minutes the music had gone to static. I'd explained again what had happened. I'd recovered sufficiently to also tell her that wacko Mike was an electronics geek and was in the middle of nowhere with a bunch of satellite dishes and radio antennas—and that Ned and he appeared to be there by themselves. Geri said she and Rose were going to make some inquiries. She was somewhat mysterious about it.

I was too shaky to puzzle about what Geri and Rose were up to. I had a large glass of milk and another toaster waffle and still felt hungry. On my way to Jaja's I stopped at Mickey D's. Chicken McNuggets, come to mama.

Jaja lived in one of the older parts of unincorporated Fresno. A lot of the houses were rentals for migrant farmworkers, who slept six or seven to a room to make the rent. In late fall, most were empty. FOR RENT signs clattered in the wind. It seemed as if every corner sported a bungalow like Jaja's, complete with a hanging sign under the eaves proclaiming FORTUNES TOLD.

This was such a mistake. Jaja was a fraud. None of this was real. I turned off the engine, then winced when I couldn't open the car door with my left hand. Well, something was real, I reminded myself, and even more real for Sirena. I found myself getting out of the car, an effort made more difficult by the wind trying to slam the door shut. Julia Madison was gibbering at me not to go in. Maddy stepped carefully up the weed-choked walk and knocked on the door.

Jaja's bungalow was painted midnight blue—an unfortunate choice on days like today where the temperature was ninety-plus. There was no air-conditioning, and I broke into a sweat the moment she closed the door behind us. The house smelled of fried onions and unchanged cat litter.

"Somehow I knew you would call," Jaja said. I followed her through a musty parlor into a small, airless room. Christ, she even had a crystal ball.

"I need help figuring something out," I said tentatively.

Jaja gestured at an ornate chair that had no padding. I perched delicately. "That's straightforward. I've found that a tarot reading is best for that. Concentrating on forces at play in a certain issue. I enjoy card readings."

I was so happy for her.

"They don't lie unless you lie to yourself," Jaja went on. "The cards can't tell you anything you don't already know, but they can really help you understand yourself and your problems better. So tell me what I can help you with. And are you going to pay with cash or credit card?"

"Um, credit card." Now that we'd dispensed with the most important issue, I launched into my somewhat incoherent spiel about a woman held captive and bad dreams.

Jaja nodded throughout as if it all made sense to her. "So you want to find this woman."

"You helped that woman at the party find her car keys."

"That's easy," she said, rolling her eyes. "She knew where they were. She just didn't know she knew."

"I have no idea where this woman is."

"Hmm. I can't really help you there. Not my forte. How about something more specific to you? About your need to find her and these bad dreams?" She reached for a deck of round cards, then put them to one side. From a small drawer in the table she drew out a more traditional looking rectangular deck of cards.

This was not going to help. Forty bucks I needed for the house payment down the drain. Plus the twenty I'd kicked in for Shandra's services. My hand ached as if it was going to fall off.

"I don't think I'll use the feminist deck for you," Jaja rattled on. "Even though you're trying to find a woman and you are a feminist." She looked at me for confirmation.

I nodded. It had been a while since I'd thought of myself as a feminist. It seemed so long ago that I had championed sisterhood on a daily basis.

"Okey-fine. Since there's something more on the mental plane going on—dreams are very much about the mind—I'm going to use this deck, which most people find very stimulating to thought."

She turned over a card for me to examine. "See? They're photo montages. This card is Strength."

An egg was centered in the card, surrounded by a lion's mane, with lionesses below it. Behind it all some eroded Greek structure loomed.

"I had a client once who thought she couldn't handle her life anymore. This card came up, and she said she'd never thought of herself being like a lion. I didn't have to do anything. She saw the lion and it spoke to her."

It wasn't speaking to me. All I saw was something anyone could search until they found something to identify with. What was mystic about that?

She asked me to shuffle the cards until "it felt right." I shuffled until I had counted to thirty, then handed them back.

She quickly dealt out ten cards with six in a cross pattern and four more to the side. She turned the cards so they were all facing me.

"This deck doesn't deal with reverses, and I've turned them so you can see better. I know them well enough to interpret even though I'm reading upside down."

All I saw was a barrage of images. A child's doll, women's faces, hands, statues, water, birds and so on.

"Wow," Jaja said. "There is lots of powerful stuff in this reading. This is going to be interesting. You are represented by the Fool-Child."

"Uh-huh."

"You're starting a journey, learning something new. See, the card is number zero, even before one. You've left behind the old you. It's a new beginning. You're inquisitive, full of emotion, intuitive, and curious about the truth."

Yeah right. So is everybody else on the planet.

"What's interesting," Jaja went on, apparently oblivious to my lack of response, "is the challenge card crossing you." She tapped a dark-hued card turned sideways across the Fool-Child. "Bondage. It's a Wand card, which means enslavement of the spirit, of energy, of psychic well-being. Look at it closely."

"I don't think I need to," I said. I hoped I looked intent at a distance.

"Julia." I looked up at Jaja. "I know you think this is garbage and all I do is rip people off. Sometimes I do." She waved her hand at the cards. "Until these cards were down I didn't know what to make of you being here. But this is a very unusual set of cards."

"I don't believe in it," I said.

"Then why are you here?"

Excellent question, and the first evidence I'd had that Jaja had any brain at all. "I don't know. I need help finding this woman."

"It can't hurt to spend twenty minutes thinking about yourself and how you might relate to this woman, would it?"

"I guess not," I said grudgingly.

Jaja smiled, and for the first time I found her remotely likable. "No refunds."

"Okay," I said, with a ghost of a smile. "Twenty minutes." I picked up the Bondage card.

The images I saw chilled me. A chain-link fence, a hawk caught in a small cage, barbed wire, handcuffs. And in one, a woman's body wrapped in bands of rope, her deep-set eyes staring out at me. I don't believe in this, I reminded myself. I put the card down as nonchalantly as I could manage, but Jaja apparently was quicker than I thought.

"A woman in bondage," she said, tapping the image. "Your challenge, the thing you must overcome to continue your journey, is the sense of being tied up, having no options. A bird can be freed, a knot cut. You have to cut your own bonds before you can cut hers."

"Okey-fine," I said. "Let's move on."

"Well, your head and heart are pretty clear. This card at the top is where your head is at. The Keeper, Woman of Crystals—she's the scientist, the deductive thinker, very much on a mental plane, which is a good place for your head to be, right? And your heart is another woman card—interesting, right? And it's the Woman of Cups, Jubilance. Ready to love, ready to dive into passionate experience."

I squirmed mentally. With Sirena's help I was diving all over the place.

"And in your immediate past, yet another woman. That's one of the reasons this reading is so interesting. There are four women cards and you got three of them. The Woman of Wands is Intuitor—Crystals is deductive, Wands is inductive. But she's in your past, someone who believes because she senses with her spirit that something is true. Gee," Jaja said, rolling her eyes. "I wonder who *that* could be."

I pursed my lips. I wasn't going to admit I was thinking of Mari. She was just my ex, and she had nothing to do with this entire situation. Except for getting me into this crazy woman's house.

"What's really interesting," Jaja enthused, "is the woman who isn't here. No Woman of Earth. She's the earth incarnate. Your problem is not on a tangible plane."

Tell that to my hand, I thought. "I see."

Jaja rolled her eyes yet again. It was practically a tic. "From here on out we talk about the future. And your future is pretty powerful. First thing I noticed is that they're all Major Arcana."

"Uh-huh."

Jaja let out an exasperated sigh. "Pay attention. This is important. Major Arcana is all about symbols and archetypes. Archetypes that are as old as thought and as pervasive as sunlight. Four of the first five cards were Minor Arcana—qualities of the archetypes in the Major Arcana, qualities you can focus and change."

"Whatever, Jaja. I'm not going to make a career of this."

"Okey-fine," she snapped. "The last five cards are not just qualities, they are the powerful forces of the archetype. Things

93

you can't control. So your future is going to be hard to control unless you work with these energies, and use them as help."

I picked up the next card. "How is the Moon going to help me?"

"Sometimes to get where we want to go we have to stick to the shadows. Not take the direct route. Use our intuition. Trust our night vision, if you will."

"Uh-huh."

"Is that all you can say? Honestly, Julia. I go months without something as interesting as this to talk to people about and all you can say is uh-huh. Fuck you."

Geez, second time today someone suggested that. "Fuck you, too, Jaja," I said, without heat. "I'm really tired, and I just want to get through this, okay?"

"Sorry I'm such a taskmaster," Jaja said. "May I remind you who called who for an appointment?"

"It seemed like a good idea at the time." So far I'd learned that my life was changing and I had to get Sirena out of bondage. I knew that when I got here.

She heaved a long-suffering sigh. "Okay. Your near future is the Moon. Working in the shadows, okay? These last four cards are outcomes. Forces in the future that will lead you to resolution. The first is what you fear or hope for. The Lovers. Are you afraid of love, or ready to embrace it?"

I ignored Jaja and studied the card. I'd seen the statue featured in it before. Two nearly identical people were wrapped in each other's arms, in major lip-lock. It was hard to tell where one ended and the other began. Looking at them from the side they appeared to share one eye between them, one mouth. Was I afraid of losing myself in Sirena?

Knock that off, I told myself sternly. Psychobabble bullshit. I picked up the next card.

"Hanged Man," Jaja said, as if its significance was plain.

"More bondage?" The central figure was hanging upside down in a sort of Christlike pose, but there was no cross.

"No, it's about one of two things. It can be about sacrifice, serious sacrifice. But it can also be about a chance to look at things from a different perspective. He's upside down, the world looks very different now. The card position is the environment you're working in. As if your day is full of different perspectives and the opportunity to look through other people's eyes."

Or Sirena's eyes. No, it was just more psychobabble. Babble, babble, babble. I realized I was babbling to myself.

"Now the next to last card is about the unexpected turn of fate. It's a person or a power you haven't taken into account as having something to do with reaching resolution. The Priestess is the repository of all knowledge and faith. She's intuitive, like the moon, but her intuition is based on knowledge you'll never understand. I'd say you are going to need to find this Priestess."

"As in there's a tall, dark and handsome woman in my future?"

Jaja looked like she wanted to smack me. "Sure, make a joke. Priestesses can be a pain. They give you answers and it's up to you to make them fit your questions."

I didn't pick Tamar's card up. Much as I didn't believe, the resemblance between the Priestess and Tamar was strong. They both had faces of stone and wild eyes.

"Well, here's your resolution card, not that you care. The Star. That's pretty positive."

The Star. Uh-huh. "So this is like the sun or something? Stars are suns."

"There's a different card for our sun. This card represents the stars, or you as a star giving your energy, heat, light to others. It's about radiating outward even if your energy has to cross great distances to reach others."

"But how is that a resolution? Go on *Star Search*?"

"I'm tired, too, Julia, okay? Maybe it's just telling you not to be a space cadet."

"I deserved that, fine." I got up and dug in my pocket for my wallet. "Here's the VISA."

Jaja took it and disappeared into the back of the house. I looked down at the cards. They were quite clever—I could look at each one and see myself or Sirena in them. It seemed as if anyone could see themselves and whatever their problem was in them.

Jaja returned with a credit-card slip for me to sign. I handed it back to her, took my credit card, and turned away.

"Julia, history is full of how stars affect our lives. You may have heard of three wise men following a star."

I glanced back at her. She was in earnest. "I'll think about it."

Jaja's bravado and hurt feelings at my stinky attitude were gone. "Maybe you're a child trying to follow a star by moonlight—that's the only time you can see them. Trust that stars are reachable."

"Have you had any nightmares lately?"

Jaja grunted. "It's the Santa Anas. Who doesn't have nightmares?"

"Nothing special recently?"

"My dreams are always special," she said. "Last night I dreamed about Jack Nicholson in *The Shining*. Here's Johnny...the ax?"

I'd only seen commercials. The ax image was interesting. "Are you a lesbian?"

"We're done, Julia." She gestured at the door. The flood of paranoia I sensed in her could only mean yes. I decided Jaja needed to spend twenty minutes with the cards asking why my question freaked her out.

I left without a good-bye. We were hardly the best of friends.

I drove home clumsily. My hand was really aching, and the bottle of Advil I kept in the glove box was empty. So was my stomach.

Whopper, onion rings, vanilla shake. As I handed my five to the person at the drive through, the wind snaked around the car and tried to wrench it out of my fingers. My left hand was so worthless that I nearly lost my grip on it. A dirt devil spun across the street and up the driveway toward the car. I rolled up the window as fast as I could but still got a noseful of dust. I had to roll down the window again to get the food, then I sneezed most of the way home.

:*Maddy—what are you doing?*:

Sirena sounded groggy.

:*Sneezing. I inhaled a bunch of dust. Damn wind.*:

:*Never stops.*: She was on the edge of sleep again.

:*Sorry I woke you.*:

:*Okay. I'm not doing too good.*:

"We're coming for you," I said. "Don't lose hope."

:*Hope.*: She fell asleep again.

I ate my burger in frustration. Another day gone, and I'd learned nothing about finding Sirena. Tamar was no closer either. I knew I had to find her—I'd known that before that silly Priestess card popped up.

When the doorbell rang it startled me out of near sleep. My shake was long melted and the onion rings stone cold.

Rose and Geri stood on the doorstep.

"What's up, girls?" I showed them into the kitchen, and they accepted my offer of coffee.

"We did a little research with people who don't like questions," Rose said when we were all settled. "Mike and Ned aren't wearing khakis, they're not militia wanna-bes. But if they're stockpiling electronics, then certain people who are stockpiling other things, well, they usually keep tabs on potential threats."

"How do you know people like this?"

Geri stared into her coffee. "Rose knows them. I'm still kind of shocked about it."

"Honey," Rose said, putting her hand on Geri's arm. "I told you when we first got together that my past was checkered." She glanced at me. "Let's just say for a while I believed that tearing things down was more productive than building them up. Then I got a little too close to one of my own creations, and when I got over the concussion I was seeing pictures in my sleep."

"Your daddy wasn't the only one in the family in the IRA?"

"I was daddy's best girl. After he died I migrated here, fell into a similar crowd. And finally fell out again."

Geri reached for Rose's hand. On Rose's side there was resolve, love, and a lot of pain. Geri was in love, too, but she was also a little scared.

"So what did you find out?"

Rose looked at Geri, who turned to me. "We found out that there's a guy who helps himself to radar imaging."

"Come again?"

"You know how there are surveillance satellites taking infrared of all our military bases?"

I didn't, but I nodded as if I did.

"Well, this guy kind of intercepts the signal. He's one of those black helicopter conspiracy theory nuts. But Rose's contacts were pretty sure he'd have accurate aerial photography of this entire area because Edwards is just to the south. So we might be able to see where someone has built a compound in the desert."

"If we get the pictures."

"We will," Rose said. "We talk a little of this guy's conspiracy junk, and he'll share."

"I don't know anything about black helicopter conspiracy theory," I said. "Remember, I work for the IRS. If anything, I'm part of the conspiracy. I make people pay taxes to pay for the black helicopters."

Rose grinned. "You might not have to talk at all. My old friend already called ahead and vouched for us."

"Me? You want me to go with you?"

"I think he'll let us look at his photos, but I doubt he'll give us copies. I only see what's happening while I'm asleep. I thought you and Sirena would be the best ones to look at pictures."

I concentrated for a moment. I heard music, but no Sirena. "She's still asleep. But I guess it couldn't hurt unless this guy is as crazy as Mike." I rubbed my hand. "Tamar called him a sick fuck, and that was *before* he stabbed Sirena's hand."

"This is going to be the best way to locate a desert

compound."

"When?" I closed my eyes wearily. "Please don't say tonight."

Geri laughed sympathetically. "Tomorrow morning. We'll pick you up around eleven. If you get a chance you might want to check out cia-helis.com."

I nodded, and they got up to leave. "Break up to make up."

Rose looked at me as if I'd lost my mind, but Geri laughed. "That's all we do. God, I hope we find that radio soon."

"I hope we find Sirena soon."

Rose kissed me on the cheek. "We all do, Julia. For all our sakes, and for hers."

I sank gratefully into bed. I listened to the wind batter the house for a few minutes, then I was asleep.

From far away I heard the door to Sirena's room open. Then Tamar's voice in Sirena's ear.

"Who are you? Why are you here?" A long silence. "I know you're one of them. Since they came I can't get any peace. I'll help you, but only if you help me first."

Sirena slept on.

Chapter 7

I eyed Rose suspiciously when she and Geri arrived just after eleven. She was wearing khaki pants and a tight T-shirt, also khaki, and clunky black boots.

"Are you supposed to be a soldier or something?"

"Or something," she said.

Geri was nervous, but committed. "I just keep telling myself she's dressed that way because she can get away with it. Khaki suits her."

It did. Rose would look great on a recruiting poster.

:Recruiting for what?:

A good question. *:For either the army, or the Lesbian Nation.:*

Sirena dabbled through my mind for explanations. She'd been subdued this morning, asking questions about what I was doing, what *Good Morning America* meant, and if I always ate animal embryos for breakfast.

:You have warriors at all times? Ready for what?:

:You're full of good questions today, aren't you?:

:Just as you're full of sarcasm this morning. Didn't you sleep well?:

I'd slept well. Too well, if that's possible. Just when I'd surface toward waking I'd sink down into another dream about Mari, or another lover. I was suspicious of Sirena's too-innocent air.

:*Do I have you to thank for the dreams?*:
:*What dreams?*:

Too innocent by far.

"Ready, Julia?"

Shit. "Sorry, guys. Sirena was a bad girl while I was sleeping."

Geri led the way to their car, a bright red Subaru Outback. She drove while Rose talked to me over the seat.

"Are you and Sirena in constant contact now?"

"Yes, pretty much."

"You look like you've lost weight."

"I do?" I looked down at my hands. "I don't feel it."

"Are you eating enough? Remember how draining Shandra said it would be?"

"I'm eating like a horse. A piggish horse."

Geri and I hummed "One of a Kind Love Affair" as we turned onto Highway 99. We drove south through Tulare, Tipton, Pixley—with the Santa Anas blowing it was all one big dust ball. The Outback was tossed around the asphalt as much as my Honda would have been. At Delano we headed east on 155. After twisting and turning enough to make me wish I'd brought some crackers, we headed north again, toward Sugarloaf Village. Long before we got there, Geri slowed, looking for a break in the roadside fencing.

"There it is," she said. "Blue Mountain Resort."

Some resort. The sign was so faded it looked like "BL AI RT." RV hookups were promised, but only a fool would take an RV up a potted dirt road. I was glad we were in a four-wheel drive.

There was no sign of civilization, but at least we were in the lee of the mountain where the wind couldn't reach us. The air seemed fresh and clear, and free of dust.

"Road twelve," Rose said, pointing. We turned off the dirt road onto another equally potted road and stopped short at a locked gate. Geri honked twice.

"What's the password?" Me and my great timing for humor.

Rose glanced over her shoulder at me. "This guy may not have much of a sense of humor, so play it cool."

"I'm cool," I said, swallowing my nerves.

A big man, with more belly than T-shirt, waddled out to unlock the gate. He looked us over, then waved us through. I hoped he believed in bathing. The T-shirt said his laundry skills left something to be desired.

Geri pulled up in front of the house.

He hollered from what looked like a small barn. "Come on into the workshop."

Rose strode directly toward him like a woman with no fear. Geri and I were a little more cautious.

"You look like Frank's type," he said to Rose.

"We're here to look at some pictures, not to gossip." Rose gestured with her head toward the barn.

"He said you were all business. Call me Jake. Go on in. I got some cold pop in the icebox."

We trooped into the barn. One corner was littered with truck parts and electronic equipment, then row after row of blueprint filing cabinets filled the rest of the space. We seemed to be headed toward a room in the back. Jake switched on a light and made good on the promise of something cold to drink—Mr. Pibb, and not no skanky diet neither.

"Now before I dig out my photos, I'm gonna assume that you're not gonna ask me how I get them."

"Wouldn't dream of it," Rose said laconically. Geri and I shook our heads in unison.

:*Sirena, pay attention.*:

:*I'm ready.*:

"You're looking for an installation of some sort, right? In the desert?"

"Right." Rose was so good at it, I was content to let her do all the talking.

"This first set is daytime shots from a couple of days ago. Different altitudes."

The pictures were roughly seventeen by seventeen and on thick photo paper. Rose had been right—we weren't going to get copies. I sorted through the first dozen or so, having no idea what I was looking for.

:Wait, Maddy. Go back.:

I turned the last picture back over and studied it. Now that I looked hard, something about it tugged my memory. I forgot Rose was doing all the talking. "Can we zoom in from this shot?"

:Zoom out.:

Out? Go higher up in the atmosphere? I remembered my thought that Sirena had been in a plane before her accident. "Wait, I want to zoom out."

Jake shrugged as if it meant no never mind to him. He sauntered out to one of the cabinets and returned with another set of photos.

The first one made me dizzy. I heard Rose inhale sharply. I knew her sketch of the checkerboard landscape would superimpose perfectly. This was where Sirena had fallen. I remembered those first few nights of nightmare, about falling toward a checkerboard. I pointed at a spot in the lower left corner. "Can we get closer pictures of a fifty-mile radius of this spot."

Mike had told Tamar they'd searched out to a fifty-mile radius for Sirena's crash site. Excitement charged through my veins. We were going to find her.

When Jake brought the next set of photos, it didn't take long for my excitement to turn to dust. Mile after mile after mile of sand, an occasional hard-packed road on the verge of being reabsorbed into the desert, and no sign of anything like a building. I wasn't sure the photos would see anything camouflaged to blend into the desert.

The three of us looked for hours while Jake wandered in and out. Finally, we admitted defeat.

"Well, I could have told you there wasn't much out there but rattlesnakes and saguaro."

He knows something that could help us, I thought suddenly. He was smug, as if he'd helped us and still outwitted us somehow.

Rose was rubbing her eyes. Geri looked thoroughly dispirited.

I don't know why I thought of Jaja, but I did. "Do you have night pictures? Infrared?" Electronics generate heat and light.

Jake's face fell. That bastard. He hadn't been going to tell us about night photos.

They were helpful—we were able to spot at least a dozen places that were inhabited, yet didn't show on the day surveillance. Rose made some notes, then turned to Jake with one of the day shots.

"Do you know what town that is?" She indicated one of the few populated areas in the radius we were examining. It wasn't very big, maybe a total of eight streets.

"Could be Yermo," he said.

Geri sighed irritably. "Yermo is off I-fifteen. That's not I-fifteen. I grew up in Barstow, for god's sake."

:Bars. Toe. Maddy, Tamar has said this. Barstow? Is that a place?:

Jubilation surged in me. "This is it. She's near Barstow."

Jake didn't bother to hide his vast masculine superiority. "Honey, there ain't nothing near Barstow except military bases and mining."

"I'll bet that's California City. It's not even big enough to be Mojave," Geri said. "The roads are right, if my memory is correct. A map would confirm it."

:Sirena? California City?:

:Not familiar. Sorry.:

:No matter. Just because they don't mention it doesn't mean it isn't close to where you are.:

Rose scribbled madly, writing down coordinates and altitudes. Her notes were dotted with sketches of mountains and roads.

"California City is a company town—military and mining. I mean what isn't a gunnery range or actual base is boron mining. Not much happens there." Geri suddenly laughed. "We used to joke that at least we didn't live in California City. When you live in Barstow it's the only place you can look down on."

104

"Julia, I want you to think hard. What night did you have the first"—Rose paused to look meaningfully at Jake—"the first communication?"

I thought about it, then had to draw myself a little calendar. "On Monday night it was two weeks." I'd had the first dream Monday night, the same dream the following night, then the first real nightmare—about hitting the ground, then waking up in bright light and being stung. It was impossible to think that Sirena had fallen for two whole days. I would have to ask her about it. And now that I thought about it, she was always evasive when I asked about the nature of the accident.

"Do you have night photos for that night? Monday night, two weeks ago?" Rose leaned back in her chair after Jake grunted and went back out to the file cabinets. "I'm just curious."

"Why night photos? She saw the checkerboard—roads, forest, a little agriculture—during the day."

Rose shrugged. "You and I dreamed at night."

Jake came back empty-handed. "No can do, ladies." He didn't sound very sorry. "There was nothing that night."

"Why not?" Rose's tone implied that she didn't believe him, but I knew Jake was telling the truth. I didn't want to think about why I was so sure of that.

"There was a big magnetic interference, photos were crap."

"Magnetic?" Geri looked at Rose, thoroughly puzzled.

Jake grunted. "Don't you remember? It was in all the papers. That big meteor shower. A bunch of space residue burned up in our atmosphere. Saw it on CNN. Shit, the government sends out helicopters to spy on all of us and no one reports anything, but a satellite or something sparkles bright and it makes the national news."

Rose was very still.

I had the oddest sensation that Sirena was holding her breath.

Rose was suddenly in motion. "You've been very helpful, Jake. I'll tell Frank he owes you."

Jake grunted. "I'd rather you owed me."

Rose didn't smile and she gestured to us to follow her back to the car. Geri lost no time getting us back to the paved road.

It was a long, silent drive back to Delano, where I sincerely hoped we'd find some food. My mind was turning over information I didn't understand. Sirena was no help whatsoever. I watched Rose chew her fingernails down to the quick and was tempted to follow suit.

JTbabe: I'm remembering my dreams now. And they aren't too bad. Rather, they're bad in a good way if you get my drift.

I got it, but wasn't about to say so.

:*You've really got to stop doing that.*:

:*Doing what?*:

VINALMOST60: I don't remember dreaming, but there is something going on that's taking my mind off my sore hand. So Sirena is somewhere near Barstow?

MaddyM: yes

roseoday: Rose is busy writing her notes over and making some sketches. she thinks she has about 12 possible locations. checking them out shouldn't take us long

MaddyM: I think we have to find Tamar first. Or try to. She's a part of this puzzle.

VINALMOST60: But we don't need her to free Sirena, do we?

MaddyM: no, probably not. But if we want Sirena to get home safely — Tamar may be her best hope.

I remembered Tamar's whispered bargain: "I'll help you, but only if you help me first." Tamar had access to money and press privileges. Who knew what she could swing for Sirena? Besides, Tamar knew something. She guarded a secret I had to know if any of this was going to make any sense to me. Damn Jaja anyway.

JTbabe: I suppose this can't wait until the weekend.

VINALMOST60: No!

roseoday: no, Sirena is in danger. Rose wants to leave tomorrow.

MaddyM: I'm ready.

JTbabe: well, I have access to a motor home. It's small, but it'll hold all of us and there's room to sleep, fridge, toilet. The necessities for fools planning to explore the desert.

roseoday: sounds divine

VINALMOST60: If we all put together a bag of groceries we can buy what we need on the way.

MaddyM: I can't believe we're on the verge of helping her, finally

JTbabe: I can't say I have the same sense of urgency that the rest of you do—I feel sort of remote. Except for the nice dreams lately.

VINALMOST60: If you saw my hand, JT...

JTbabe: I know.

roseoday: JT, right now I'm hearing Live and Let Die for the second time this week. A few minutes ago it was Say Has Anybody Seen My Sweet Gypsy Rose. And before that it was sing, sing a song, sing out loud, sing out strong

JTbabe: Stop. That's torture enough! =)

No kidding. Geri hadn't even mentioned "Behind Closed Doors"—a song guaranteed to turn the stomach of any lesbian.

roseoday: I checked this music. there hasn't been anything later than 1973. can anyone think why that date might be important? what happened in 73?

VINALMOST60: The Energy Crisis. Picasso died.

JTbabe: I was 11. I kissed my best friend.

MaddyM: I was born in 1973. don't know if that's significant.

roseoday: I was born in 75, so maybe not

VINALMOST60: I have a chronology reference. Why don't I do a digest and send it along in a little while?

roseoday: Vina, you're amazing.

VINALMOST60: Thank you. I don't think this is going to help us.

roseoday: Rose and I were talking about maybe the music being on a shortwave. Like Mike's ego could be big enough to think his musical choices should be heard by his neighbors, but he's not big enough to blast it very far

MaddyM: could be. Course when we get to Barstow we can hunt the dial again.

roseoday: that's right. my calls didn't include stations that far south. but it's mostly country music out that way.

MaddyM: now you're torturing me

JTbabe: there's nothing wrong with country music!

MaddyM: to each her own, just not my cup of tea

JTbabe: hmph

VINALMOST60: Pax. I'll sign off now and go do the digest.

The screen cleared, and I wobbled off to make some more food. When we'd arrived home Rose had commented again that I seemed thinner. I had studied myself in the bathroom mirror— and then stepped on the scales. She was right. I'd lost nearly four pounds in the last week. My eyes looked bigger, and my cheekbones were prominent. When I did go back to work, Emily would have no trouble believing I had been sick.

Lebanon bologna and Triscuits. Yum.

:*So sleepy.*:

:*Don't fight it. Save your strength. We'll be near you tomorrow.*:

Sirena's reaction was an odd mixture. I sensed her elation, and then something else. Trepidation.

:Maddy, I haven't told you everything.:
:Like I didn't know that already.:
:I should tell you.:
:When I see you is soon enough. Nothing you could say or do is going to stop me from getting to you. I have to help you if I'm ever going to respect myself again. So go to sleep. Tell me tomorrow, if you must.:
:Okay. So sleepy.:

My computer pinged with received mail, and I printed the file Vina had enclosed. I devoured a can of ravioli and another bowl of cereal while I read Vina's summary.

Interesting year, 1973. After most of the antiwar protests, before disco. The average single family home sold for $28,900. Oil and grain shortages triggered a worldwide recession. The UPC bar code made its first appearance, as did nutrition labels. Nixon froze retail food prices. *Burr, Breakfast of Champions* and *Fear of Flying* were all published. I'd read *Breakfast of Champions* a long time ago.

Agnew resigned, Nixon pulled the troops out of Vietnam, but didn't stop bombing Cambodia. Haldeman and the rest resigned in the midst of Watergate. Juan Perón returned to Argentina after eighteen years of exile. The Yom Kippur War broke out, with arms and other support supplied by the US and Russia on opposite sides, of course. Nearly twenty thousand people died in eighteen days of fighting. The Supreme Court handed down *Roe v. Wade*.

Turning to sports—Vina didn't ignore anything—Miami beat Washington in the Super Bowl, The A's took the World Series from the Mets, and Secretariat won the Triple Crown. Billie Jean King wiped Bobby Riggs's tiny little butt all over a tennis court in the Astrodome.

Mean Streets, Paper Moon and *American Graffiti* were tops at the movies. The Skylab III astronauts spent almost sixty days in space, and Pioneer 10 transmitted pictures of Jupiter from within eighty-one thousand miles of its spinning surface.

Vina added a note that there was of course a lot more, but

she'd mostly concentrated on topics of interest to Americans.

My head was swimming. This was just like the idea that only lesbians might be in link with Sirena. A great big So What. So whoever ran the music had a fixation with 1973. Maybe they just didn't like anything more recent. My mother personally hasn't listened to the radio since Elvis went off the charts.

I toddled off to bed, suddenly eager to fall asleep. I hoped Sirena wouldn't fiddle with my dreams again tonight, at least not enough for everyone else to know about it. I prodded her in my mind—she was out cold. So I told myself I was probably in for uninterrupted sleep.

I was wrong.

First off, I knew I wasn't dreaming. I mean I was dreaming, but they weren't my dreams. After a while I realized they had to be Sirena's, and filtered through whatever sedative was in the IV.

She walked underwater through rooms with mother-of-pearl walls. They shimmered in peach-toned light. She increased her pace—she was eager to reach the end.

Sounds I couldn't follow, notes of music, then a wonderful swell of happiness. All I'd known through her was despair and anger, and this felt so good. She sailed through a doorway and was swept into someone's arms.

They rolled together, squealing and giggling. No words were spoken, and yet they laughed and communicated. The other person stood up and seemed ten feet tall. It was an older woman, her face creased with joy and understanding. I suddenly recognized the feelings these two were sharing back and forth— welcome, I love you, and I've missed you, and plainly the older woman asked Sirena to tell her all about it.

Sirena's mother—it must have been. Even as Sirena glanced at herself I noticed her feet were smaller, her legs shorter. A dream about childhood, when everything is safe, when your mother loves you, when everything you do and say is important to her.

There was a rush of noise at the doorway, and Sirena

somersaulted—easy to do, underwater—into the midst of newcomers. A round of hugs, flashes of coral-tinted limbs, then a half dozen pairs of brightly gleaming eyes turned on Sirena. Those same emotions washed over her—welcome, we love you, and we've missed you. Six girls in white jumpsuits, like school uniforms, gathered around her. Sirena's mother joined them, and I wanted to cry. They were a family and there was so much love, love like I'd never known.

Her dream was slipping away. Was it a homecoming in her past, or the one she hoped for in the future?

Her dream eyes opened on a new doorway. Her body thrilled with excitement. She stepped out of a...bus, some sort of transport. And everywhere she looked were women in white, peach, red and blue jumpsuits. Some played a game with a deep purple ball, and others sat talking on lush grass that looked more blue than green. A college campus? The ages seemed right. One young woman, reclining on the grass, opened her eyes when Sirena stopped next to her. They exchanged emotions, ideas—but no words. The woman on the grass smiled and reformed into a bed, no she was on a bed. The light was gone and there was only this lovely woman, long-limbed and deeply tanned, her platinum hair and eyes gleaming in the darkness.

Sirena's body was searingly alive, and her arousal was more powerful than my own had ever been—at least until that night with JT. She reached down, her fingers in wet, slick heat I knew so well. Her fingers stirred through curves of welcoming flesh and found resistance in muscles that pushed back, then quivered and gave way.

Their anticipation rose together, their bodies seemed to merge into one, a blur of sensation. Sirena floated and turned in the air—dreams are wonderful that way. No creaking knees, cramping hips or grunts in this dream. She nudged Platinum's knees apart with her nose and my breath caught as I felt Platinum doing the same to Sirena. They blended again until all I could see was a shimmering, brilliant light that grew impossibly bright, then winked out.

I knew my own body was responding to the pressure of Platinum's mouth, to the vicarious taste and scent of Platinum on Sirena's mouth. They/we rolled together through a warm, liquid darkness. Just like the love of her family had been foreign to me, so was this all-consuming erotic pulse, beating to the exclusion of all thought. Anticipation rose, aching toward satisfaction. Every part of me that had ever longed to be touched, licked, caressed, was pleasured exactly how I needed it, exactly how I wanted it, while my tongue, fingers, teeth and lips all gave what was needed, exactly how I could give it, all of it was happening all at once and then I realized the goal was not satisfaction, it was this perfect moment of balance. We hung suspended on the brink of I don't know what, and the dream stayed there for what seemed like hours, as if climax was not a crest, but a deep ocean to be sailed for as long as the energy lasted.

I had enough sense of self to realize I was not in the dream, only experiencing it as Sirena did. But I knew my own body was quivering with ecstasy, like it was my first time.

:First time...:

:We're dreaming.:

:If you say so.: Sirena seemed to turn and face me, but all I saw was Platinum's eyes. *:That is me.:*

:You? I thought it was your lover.:

:No, me. You're not looking through my eyes, Maddy. You're looking through your own.:

Her mouth looked bruised with desire. I told myself I should be scared.

:Kiss me, Maddy.:

I filled my hands with her soft, platinum hair, and I found myself drifting into the twinkling stars of her eyes. *:We're dreaming.:*

:If you say so.:

I kissed her.

I no longer knew where I ended and she began. I no longer

cared. She filled me with sensation, sex and orgasm and starting over. When it seemed our kisses were finally less fervent, she held me and let me look into her memories, and she filled me with even more precious sensations—welcome, I love you, I've missed you.

I discovered that for thirty-plus years I'd told myself the biggest lie of all—that I knew what it meant to be alive. I'd never known, not until now, when Sirena cradled me in her dreams and we sighed with shared breath. When I opened my eyes my bedroom seemed bright as day, but the night was only half over.

:Come back.: Sirena's whisper made me close my eyes.

:Kiss me.:

Chapter 8

Barstow isn't just in the middle of nowhere. You have to get to the middle of nowhere before you can head east to Barstow.

The motor home creaked along State Route 58 somewhere between Tehachapi and Mojave, rocking as gusts of air from passing trucks blew us toward the side of the road while the wind buffeted us toward oncoming traffic. JT was a capable driver, but I didn't know about the overall stability of the motor home, which had seen better days. Zigzagging was not my favored mode of travel.

I had finally slept by myself, and Sirena was not answering me yet this morning. I could hear the radio ("Angie"), but Sirena was deeply asleep. With just a little effort I could believe that last night had been just a dream. Just wishful thinking. But it hadn't been, and that reality scared me. I'd given myself with all my aching soul to Sirena. What would I do when I finally saw her, when we finally touched in the flesh? What would I do when we met, and then said good-bye? Tamar would take her away. I grew more certain of that with every mile we traveled.

Rose was keeping JT company in the cab while Vina dozed on the little sofa on one side of the motor home. Geri had the forward-facing bench at the table. Her gaze was on the magazine in her hands, but she hadn't turned a page in almost fifteen minutes. I looked out the window at the passing scrub and hedgehog cactus, occasionally seeing an ocotillo or yucca plant to break up the monotony.

Since I was facing backward, I could only see where we had been, not where we were going. Like my life, I thought. Always looking at the past, and never looking ahead. I decided to take accounting in college because I was looking back at my childhood and longing for anything different from my mother's dependence on men for survival. Boyfriends and jobs came and went with equal rapidity. She'd declare herself independent of men, then money would get tight and she'd find a new boyfriend to pay the bills for a while.

By the time I was fifteen I didn't even learn their names. I didn't want to know who was trying the knob of my bedroom door and cursing quietly when he found it locked. And my mother had started telling me that none of them stayed because of my sullenness. She drank more; I talked less.

I went out waitressing myself to get the fees for my first semester of college, then found my mother expected me to help with the expenses since I could work. College was a waste of time, she told me. I needed to learn how to type and then I'd have a decent job where my butt didn't get pinched every day.

I looked back at my childhood and decided to become an accountant. Then I looked back at the misery of working almost forty hours a week and carrying a full class load and decided I wanted a life with more leisure, which meant more money. My grades were good enough to get me a job in a medium-size accounting firm in San Jose, and I wiped the disappointment and grime of Aptos off my shoes forever.

I looked back on four years of slaving harder than I thought possible in an accounting firm, trying to get into the consultant track where the big money was. I'd finally realized I was going to kill myself if I didn't make a change and that the men who owned the firm had no intention of allowing any woman to climb into their club—except on her back, maybe. I weighed the least I ever had in my life, an unhealthy 108, and I was constantly fighting a cold. Mari had suggested that it was bad air in the office building when I'd told her about it. I thought it more likely my diet of M&M's and cola had something to do with it.

Looking back at those wasted years is why I sought a civil service job with plannable hours and a finite set of knowledge to work with. I was happy at the IRS, but I knew that I was there because of the past, not because of a future I'd ever dreamed of. I'd never looked ahead in my life, never envisioned myself settling down, never thought about what I'd like from a home.

Mari had said that I probably felt this way because of internalized homophobia. I didn't think about a happy future because I didn't think I deserved one. It was one of the few times I ever said bullshit aloud to Marigold's bullshit. Realizing I was a lesbian had been completely liberating—the most joyful moment of my life. It opened my horizons. We'd had a colossal fight. Making up had been memorable.

I didn't know what the future was going to bring me. I was realizing I'd never conceived of having a future any different from last year or the year before. I was as bad as my mother in that respect.

No doubt Jaja would say that until recently I hadn't believed in the things that would make up my future, and therefore my future was invisible to me. Was this journey, in a dilapidated motor home fighting the vicious Santa Ana winds, clogged with trucks and soot and dust—was this the road to the future?

Could my future have Sirena in it? Was she The Star?

"What are you thinking about?"

I started, then smiled ruefully at Geri. "Nonsense, mostly."

"Rose is right, you know."

"About what?"

"You're thinner. But—you know when you walked into the classroom on Saturday I thought you were one of the unhappiest people I'd ever seen. You seemed so...depressed. Believe me, I know the signs. You can't teach high school and not know when someone is depressed. I can also tell when someone is happy—and I'd say you're happy right now." She glanced meaningfully around the motor home. "Well, feeling a little trepidation, perhaps, as are we all. But you're happy."

Was it only Saturday that I'd met Geri and Rose, and Vina and JT? It seemed an eternity now. "What I know is that I'm scared. Not of what's ahead—well, a little of that. Because I don't know what's going to happen when we find her. But I'm really scared that this freaked-out situation is going to be the high point of my entire life. I have no idea what my life will be like when this is over. I can't for the life of me picture myself going back to nine-to-five paper pushing."

"You'll be a different person," Geri said. "Maybe you'll see new opportunities. Change is a good thing because you can look at yourself differently."

"Like hanging upside down," I said.

Geri looked confused. How could I enlighten her?

"Pit stop," JT yelled. "We're coming into Mojave. We need gas. I think we burned half a tank just climbing the Tehachapi Pass. My friend Esther told me to never let it get below a quarter tank."

As soon as we stopped moving the temperature inside the motor home skyrocketed. I offered to go inside to pay for the gas from our collective kitty. The asphalt was soft from the heat. Any part of me not already perspiring sprang into action. The wind deposited a fine layer of red dust on my bare arms and face, and my hair instantly felt grimy.

At least it's a dry heat, I thought, then found I was too dispirited to do more than grimace.

Geri had made sandwiches and once we were underway again I ate every bite under her watchful eye. A bag of chips, a Coke and I was almost not hungry any more. The air whipping through the window screens dried the sweat on my face and arms, but left the dirty feeling behind.

"I know it must be a million degrees up there," Geri said, pointing at the overcab bed, "but you should try to get some sleep. You look like the wind is going to knock you over, and the bed down here is in the sun now."

That was a sad comment on my health, coming from petite Geri. The built-in couch where Vina had been resting was now in the sun, and closing the blinds would cut off the air supply—unthinkable. I was too weary to argue. I struggled into the bunk, bruising my pelvis and wrenching my still tender hand in the process.

I did try to sleep, and when that seemed impossible—the heat, mostly—I tried to contact Sirena.

The Isley Brothers were asking, "Who's that lady?" I zeroed in quickly and knew we were closer because it seemed so easy.

:*You're awake, I know you are.*:

Sirena pushed me away. Well, she tried to.

:*What's wrong? I'm not going away, so you can stop that.*:

:*I forgot who I was. Last night. And who you were.*:

:*Does it matter that much? Sirena, I have no regrets.*:

:*I shouldn't have done that. It was wrong. Unethical.*:

:*You're not my therapist.*:

:*It is wrong, where I'm from.*:

:*Well, you're in my country at the moment, and I don't think we've got a law on the books about what we did last night. Not even in Georgia.*:

She couldn't help herself, and I actually reveled in her quick search of my mind for information on Georgia and sodomy laws.

:*Your lawgivers are occupied with trivial things.*:

:*Tell me about it. Look, I'm confused about something.*:

:?:

:*Well, when you asked me what a lesbian was you said you weren't familiar with the concept because you have fewer options where you're from.*:

I felt her laughter. :*My home is occupied only by women. So we have no word to differentiate us from an option that doesn't exist. Would you need the word homosexual if there was no heterosexuality?*:

:*What a trip! You mean somewhere on this messed up planet there's a society of women? What are you, Amazons?*:

While Sirena absorbed the concept of Amazons, I looked down at Geri and Rose, sitting as close together as the heat would allow. It didn't look as if the landscape had changed much. I scooted to the edge of the bunk and hung my head over far enough to look out through the windshield. Upside down the sky was made of asphalt with the familiar tan and red sand on the left and right. Off in the distance to the north were...I mentally tried to turn the image over. White snow cones upside down were... mountains. Mountains of white.

:*We are not Amazons, not as you mean it. But...we are similar. Maddy, I have to tell you something*—:

"Stop! Pull over!" I nearly broke my ankle clambering down out of the bunk.

"Shit, Julia," JT was saying. "You nearly scared me to death." She was guiding the motor home onto the shoulder. I had the door open before we were fully stopped. When I jumped out onto the hard-packed sand I was engulfed in the dust we'd stirred up.

Coughing, I leaned back into the motor home. "Rose, come and look."

The dust cleared, and in the hazy, shimmering distance were mountains of white.

"It's them," Rose whispered.

Sirena had run across desert, looking for water. She'd thought the white mountains were covered with snow. They weren't even mountains, just huge mounds of boron from the nearby mining operations. But from here, on a flat desert landscape with the eye-tricks of dancing heat, they looked like mountains.

I darted across the highway so I could study the landscape without cars and trucks ruining my concentration. The sand had the hard, crusted quality I remembered from the dream. I walked forward for a minute or so, heeding Vina's plea to be careful and watch for snakes.

I ignored the sound of traffic and looked to the west. The horizon was unbroken by roads or structures, and I could almost see the black figures pursuing Sirena across this barren landscape, too far from the highway for Sirena to have ever seen it. All her concentration had been on reaching the white mountains.

I turned back and something stung my hand. I let out a startled yelp, then realized I'd brushed up against the huge paddle of a low cactus. I rubbed the back of my hand and then smiled ruefully. Another piece of the puzzle.

"Look," I said to Vina when I rejoined the group. Little red pinpricks dotted the back of my hand. "Seem familiar?"

"A cactus?"

"She must have fallen onto one."

Sirena said, quite grumpily, :*Well, I was dizzy at the time.*:

JT gestured at the mounds of boron. "So you think she what—crashlanded? Somewhere near here?"

"And then she ran toward the boron mines, and they caught her somewhere near them. I guess it could be some other similar vista, but it's all in this vicinity. All the little details match up."

"How long was she transported?"

I looked at JT in something like awe. "You're very practical, did you know that?"

Her look said she wasn't overwhelmed by my flattery.

"I'm not joking. I would have never thought of that. She was transported, after dark, for about three hours. I dreamed about being bounced around. I blacked out when it ended."

Vina was nodding. "Me, too. It was a night I didn't get more than three hours of sleep. And it was all the sensations Julia described."

Rose had her sketches of Jake's photos. "So on this kind of terrain, after dark, you could do, what, thirty miles an hour? Being bounced doesn't sound like they used the road."

"More like twenty. There aren't exactly streetlights," JT said. "So they are within sixty miles or so of here."

Geri scrambled inside, and we all followed suit. It was sweltering, but an improvement over standing in the relentless sun and wind.

She spread the Triple-A map on the table. "We're about here, right JT?"

JT nodded, then pointed at the turnoff to California City we'd passed five miles back. "Are you sure we don't need to go up there?"

Rose nodded slowly. "I really don't think we'll find anything."

"Tamar is in Barstow, or she passed through Barstow on her way to where Sirena is. We need to go there. We need to find Tamar." I was certain of this.

:*Maddy, I need to tell you something.*:

:*What?*:

She hesitated, and I got annoyed. :*Look, either tell me or give it a rest. Do you think we're on the right track?*:

:*Yes.*:

"Sirena thinks we're on the right track," I reported.

JT jangled the keys. "Well then, let's get going again."

Geri and I pored over the map while I demolished most of a box of Hostess Cupcakes. I knew that Sirena had something to tell me, and whatever it was would change things—if it wasn't something big she would have told me already. But I felt as if I'd just gotten a handle on things. She could tell me tonight, while I was sleeping.

Barstow was bigger than I had thought it was. We creaked down First Avenue, across the mud-choked Mojave River, then into the main drag of town called, not unsurprisingly, Main Street.

There were also more motels than I had expected. I'd hoped we would be able to canvass them for a recent guest named Tamar

Reese. We still could, but it would take longer. It would be easier if she were actually staying there now, but I knew she was at the compound with Ned and Mike.

We pulled into a crowded, windblown, sun-beaten KOA, then plodded to the coffee shop just down the street. Sandwiches had been too long ago for me, and the smell of food made me weak. Fortunately, the restaurant's air-conditioning was in good shape. My body temperature dropped at least five degrees while we waited on sticky seats for a table to accommodate all of us. Geri and JT both muttered about the lack of cell phone service, then pocketed their phones when the waitress signaled our table was ready.

When I stood up I wobbled, and JT was quickly there.

"I'm okay."

"I know." She took my arm, and I didn't resist.

Food was within reach. I didn't know why I was so out of it, except that maybe Sirena seemed out of it, too. Maybe they'd stepped up her sedatives or something.

I ordered the dinner that came with the most mashed potatoes, which was an open-face turkey sandwich.

"Order something else," JT said.

"I want this." I sounded like a mulish child, but who did JT think she was?

Patiently, she explained, "I think you should order something additional. More protein, too."

Rose quickly echoed JT's suggestion, so I ordered a French dip and a bowl of clam chowder. Comfort food heaven.

The service was slow, which suited our mood. We were all drained from the heat and driving and carefully not talking about the future. JT shared her hopes for a change in her nursing assignment from geriatrics to psych. Vina had been overseeing the upgrading of the computer system at the library. Geri would be glad if the substitute got her kids through any of the lesson plans she'd left, while Rose admitted she missed the mindless repetition of cashiering at a grocery store.

"It's not in the least creative, but it does clear the mind," she said.

"Like calculating tax and penalties," I said. "It's not rocket science, but the world goes away when I get into it. When this first happened I used tax code to shut it down. I don't think that would work now."

The waitress dropped off my clam chowder and Rose's chef salad. I had to shake my head slightly to shake off a wave of dizziness, then I applied all my concentration to eating. There was no need for small talk. After years of awkward interaction with people, always suspecting they found me odd or wanting, it was nice to be comfortable. Because we were sharing this experience our differences didn't matter. So far the only serious one appeared to be a three to two split on Diet Coke versus Diet Pepsi.

I finished the soup, then ate the saltines that had come with it. "I think they stepped up Sirena's sedative. I feel...loopy."

"Loopy?" JT arched an eyebrow.

"A bit dizzy," Vina said, closing her eyes briefly. "Just a bit dizzy."

"Why would they be sedating her more?"

I shook my head. "I don't know. When we get back to the motor home, I'll try to ask her. I can't do it now." I glanced around the crowded restaurant.

"Time enough this evening," Rose said. "We'll have nothing but time. I'm glad I brought cards. How lovely, five insomniacs in a motor home in ninety degrees."

"Good lord." JT was both amused and disbelieving. "I never thought I'd be here."

"Neither did I." To my relief the turkey sandwich arrived, and I stuffed myself, finishing the last drop of gravy and every bit of the instant mashed potatoes. When the French dip came I finished that, too. It was not even sliced beef, but the cheaper formed stuff. I soaked it in the so-called *au jus*, which tasted exactly like bouillon from cubes. It was delicious.

123

"Feeling better?" JT made eye contact with me for what felt like the first time since that night together. All at once I was in that memory, heard her gasping and my pleading.

"Yes." My heart was pounding.

"That's good." Her upper lip trembled ever so slightly. "Have dessert."

I sublimated my arousal with a hot fudge sundae. It was delicious.

We played canasta, then gin, then pinochle. The kerosene lantern gave excellent light. Sitting outside at the picnic table was infinitely better than the air inside the motor home even if it meant swatting sand fleas and horse flies.

The campground was almost deserted, so we talked more freely than we had in the restaurant. As we played cards, Rose laid out a plan for locating the various complexes we'd seen on Jake's surveillance photos. I couldn't be sure, but I was hopeful that when we got close to Sirena I'd know and we wouldn't have to concoct some sort of story to take a look around at every single place.

JT went into the motor home for some chips and sodas. She dropped a can on her way down the steps, and it rolled behind the rear wheels.

"I'll get another one," she said. "We can look for it in the morning."

"It's right there." I pointed.

"Right where?" She peered in the direction I was pointing.

"Behind the wheel." I got up and retrieved the can.

"How could you see that?" JT blinked. "I can hardly see the cards, let alone something that far away."

"It was plain as day." I shrugged. "Late desert sunsets, I guess." Why did everyone look so puzzled? "What?"

Vina put down her cards. "Julia, the sun went down just after we got back here. It's been down for several hours now."

"No way," I said, shaking my head. "It's so bright." I looked toward the west—and there was no sun, and no twilight. Yet everything around me was illuminated with a persistent, flat light.

I carefully stood up and examined the night sky. If there was a moon it hadn't risen yet. I swallowed hard, then studied the puzzled faces of my companions. "I seem to have a new skill," I said with a steady voice.

"You can really see, like it was day?"

I nodded. "Just about. Night vision." I looked up. "The stars seem so close."

"That's the elevation," Geri said.

I didn't disagree, but I knew I was seeing more of them than I ever had, and I knew their properties. Names and facts from a long-forgotten astronomy class popped up. Altair was in the heart of the sky, twinkling with blue energy. An arc of planets spilled toward me, Pluto, Venus, Mars, then Neptune, Uranus and Jupiter much lower, with Saturn almost at the horizon. Jupiter glowed magnificently red.

The moon would rise soon, and with it Sirius. The stars swirled over me, and I felt as if I could dream a ladder to climb into their dance. I knew how to do it, if only I could get away, if only I could free my hands. But my hands were free...I stretched up, wrists together, fingers fanned out...it was so...easy.

Next thing I knew, JT was patting my face with a cold washcloth. She reported that I was coming around.

"You went over backward," she told me. "Are you hurt?"

"No." I was puzzled. "What happened?"

"You tell me." She was leaning over me, and it would have taken only a moment's effort to put my arms around her. I ached for the contact of skin.

I closed my eyes. What was wrong with me?

"I think Julia would be better off inside," Vina said. "And I'm going to lie down, too. *Loopy* is the best word for this... sensation."

"She's drugged," I mumbled. "I mean more than before."

JT helped me up, and Geri offered her hand from inside. Rose had been busy making up the built-in couch with sheets.

"Geez, I feel like royalty or something," I said. Everyone was waiting on me.

"You scared the shit out of me," Rose said. "If you're going to step onto The Road like that, you need to be sitting down with someone watching over you. You could have easily stopped breathing."

"I wasn't on any road." I stretched out on the cool sheets and my eyes closed by themselves. I smiled. "But I was certainly going somewhere."

Softly, Rose asked, "But to where?"

I didn't know the answer.

I could hear them talking in low voices. After a while the lights went out, with only the low rustlings of everyone settling in. I opened my eyes slightly; I could see perfectly. Geri and Rose were in the overcab bed, which was too small for two people who weren't lovers. Vina was on the bed created by lowering the table, and JT was stretched out on top of a sleeping bag on a thick foam pad on the floor. Cozy. I closed my eyes and let the heat and the dizziness overwhelm me.

:This is so strange. I feel like I've taken twelve Percodan or something.:

:I couldn't reach you.: Sirena was groggy. *:Not while you were awake.:*

:I'm here now.: Tower of Power intoned "So Very Hard to Go" while I tried to concentrate. *:I really am asleep, aren't I?:*

:We both are, I guess. Maddy, it's hard to think.:

:I know. Save your strength.:

:I want to tell you the truth now.:

:The truth isn't important right now. Tell me tomorrow when we find you. Just rest now. Relax.:

:How can I when you are so close? I can feel your mind caressing mine. I feel...like I want you to touch me, but I know you can't. You're too far away.:

126

:After last night, can you have any doubts that I want to touch you?:

:I know, but—:

The door to Sirena's room flew open, and Ned banged his way in. My heart went into my throat as I jerked in my sleep.

"That damn bitch," he was grousing. "And Mr. Lord Almighty telling me I'll take her back to town like I'm some sort of taxi. I'm gonna push her out of the car at sixty miles an hour. No one will ever find her bones."

Little man with big boasts to cover his tiny masculinity. He was in a foul mood, that was for sure. He slammed something down on the table near Sirena, who was willing herself not to react.

"She and Mike can have their little private talk. I know what Mike's after. He ain't gonna get it, not from that cold-assed bitch."

The stench of his unwashed body was tickling at Sirena's nose. I swallowed hard, fighting down my gag reflex. Smells were the strongest triggers of memory, my therapist had told me. He smelled like boyfriend number four, who equated body odor with virility. I'd thrown up on his pants—not precisely the experience he'd been looking for.

"I oughta give it to her good. Shut her up. Yapping at me like she's got a right." I could tell he was standing next to Sirena now because the foul smell got stronger. He fondled her breasts, his actions more obscene for their casualness.

Sirena was trying to push me out of her head, but either I was stronger than I thought or she was too drugged to succeed.

:You've been through enough. Wake up, go away.:

:I won't leave you to him. The worst times were when I couldn't be somewhere else. Think of your mother, your sisters. Think of a vacation, a holiday. Be somewhere else for now.:

Ned was breathing hard, one hand on Sirena's breast, one hand on himself. My rage was white-hot. I think if I'd been able to reach him at that moment I'd have killed him.

127

:Once when I was little, my mother took us to a ballet. I remember how beautiful the costumes were. I wanted to be a dancer.:

:What happened to that dream?:

:Reality. I wasn't good enough to be a performer and I'm grateful I figured it out on my own before I was too old to concentrate on something else. My youngest sister, now she's a dancer. I haven't seen her in such a long time.: A wave of sadness threatened to bring Sirena back to Ned's fumblings.

:What was the ballet about?: Sirena knew nothing of men. I gave Ned about thirty more seconds.

:A child falls asleep and is entertained by the Queens of the Hours. They dance for her, they sing. She is given a great gift and then wakes up, dancing.:

:What kind of gift?: Ned was done. He wiped Sirena's arm and shoulder, but I could still feel the sticky slime. I could smell it, even after he covered her and stepped away. The sound of his zipper was like fingernails on a chalkboard.

:It was different every performance. Sometimes she saw the face of her life-mate, and sometimes she learned the names of her children or experienced her calling. And she always danced. I wanted to be her.:

Ned left, and I began to surface out of sleep.

:Dream about being her, my darling. I'll be back soon. It's only the drugs that make me seem so far away.:

:Hurry back.:

It would take me a while to fall asleep again. It would be the same for all of us. We didn't speak, but I think we all knew we were awake and why. I didn't need to open my eyes to see Vina's tears and JT's anger, or to know that Geri cradled Rose in helpless comfort.

Chapter 9

We planned to do our desert hunting in the relatively cool morning. It made sense with the temperature over ninety at nine A.M., so we creaked back to Route 58, then turned east to Yermo and Calico Ghost Town.

We started there because three installations were within twenty miles of each other, and a fourth was another twenty miles out, toward long-dry Coyote Lake. They were all within fifty to seventy miles of the boron mines. We were driving in a big circle. I hoped that wasn't a metaphor for our day.

I hoped we would be able to get back into Barstow by late afternoon. We could start looking for Tamar then. Ned was bringing her back to town sometime during the day, and none too happy about it. It would be hilarious if we passed them on the road, but that kind of coincidence was not in our future—of that I was certain. The day was too hot and the wind too choking for simple solutions.

The first cluster of buildings that came up out of the desert turned out to be a U.S. Geological Society installation, and it looked unoccupied. It also wasn't really a compound, just housing for what appeared to be weather tracking equipment.

As we drove toward the next site, Vina wondered if we wouldn't save heat stroke and a lot of gas by visiting the county assessor's office.

"Hard to say," Rose said. "We'd call attention to ourselves. And who knows who owns what land out here. Mike could be leasing from a mining company, and we'd never know."

I could tell that the need for a modicum of stealth bothered Vina, but she accepted—as did I—that we really had no choice. Only we understood what we were all collectively experiencing. Someone who wasn't in some sort of link with Sirena would think we were certifiable.

We limped back into Barstow in the midafternoon, dust-weary and dehydrated, despite drinking every liquid we'd brought with us. The farther out we'd driven the more I had known we weren't any closer to Sirena and the more severe the wind seemed to be. Sites two and three had been within Fort Irwin's confines, and the fourth an outlying cluster of buildings from the Calico Mountains archeological dig. After a cold drink and some food we were going to canvass motels for Tamar Reese.

Tomorrow, if it came to that, we'd check the remaining sites to the west of Barstow. No one, including me, was thrilled at the prospect of another day in the heat and grit.

I tried to get through to Sirena, but she just wasn't there. The music was on—Donny Osmond's "The Twelfth of Never." And I thought Tony Orlando was nauseating. Then "Little Willy" got stuck in my head.

The music and the heat weren't the worst part of the day for me. It was knowing we were spinning our wheels and clearly sensing the dwindling spirits everyone was trying so hard to hide. Every twenty-four hours left Sirena in the control of men who would use her and didn't seem to care that she was slowly dying in captivity. They'd not let her up to walk for days and days.

We found a gas station with a bank of pay phones and slowly, taking turns standing in the relentless sun and wind, we called every motel in the book asking for Tamar Reese. Meanwhile, JT trundled off in the motor home for ice, beverages, snacks and gas.

None of the motels had ever heard of Tamar Reese. Vina kept track of the no answers or ones who wouldn't tell us if she was staying there. Her tidy list in hand, we set out to visit each of the no-tells personally to see if we could get an answer.

From the passenger seat I watched Geri come out of the last motel. From her walk I could tell she'd had no luck. Tamar Reese was either not registered under her name or she wasn't in Barstow. Geri had thought Yermo extremely unlikely, but we'd have to try there next.

I wanted my dinner. I wanted this to be over. I wanted Sirena to wake up. I couldn't believe another day was gone and we'd discovered nothing.

Off to Yermo we went. A campground there boasted a pool, and it sounded like a slice of heaven to all of us, even if we didn't find Tamar. The sun was beginning to droop behind the horizon when we drove into the little town. It was as small as a town could be and still be a town. Three streets, a minimart, two motels, one coffee shop and a campground. One of the motels, the coffee shop and the campground were all part of the same parcel proudly emblazoned "The Oasis."

Vina volunteered to canvass the two empty-looking motels for Tamar. She returned with a discouraged face and another bag of ice—we'd polished off most of the one JT had bought on the drive. Five minutes later we were all in the small pool. We had it to ourselves, which made it easier to go in wearing T-shirts—none of us had planned for something as frivolous as swimming.

I floated on the water and relaxed. The heat of the day seeped out of my body. Every once in a while I'd submerge, liking the quiet. I had a harder time telling what the others were feeling while I was underwater, which was a relief. Night vision was kind of handy, I mused. I could see underwater really well.

:Madddddddy.:

:Sirena, you're awake?:

131

:Maddddddy.:

I stood up—the water was only five feet. *:Sirena, I'm here.:*

Nothing. I couldn't hear her anymore. Rose swam by, a bundle of determination and resolve. I wondered if the quiet of underwater had helped me hear her, so I went under again.

:Maddddddy...:

She was calling me, but I sensed it was in her own dreams that she called. She twisted her head from side to side for a moment, then shivered.

:Maddddddy, hellllppp me....:

Her dreams were not peaceful. I surfaced, gasping for air. I had been wondering about what Tamar had said to Mike—about animals in captivity going nuts. But Sirena was not an animal, and I knew her incoherence was probably whatever Mike was putting into her IV.

:I'm coming, darling. I'll be with you as soon as I can.: I knew she couldn't hear me, but I felt better.

Greatly refreshed, I slipped back into my shorts and a clean shirt for dinner. Swimming had left me trembling with hunger. I did my best to ignore the sense of futility that I knew was dogging all of us.

"At least I like this song." Geri's voice was muffled as she pulled her Teachers-Do-It-With-Class T-shirt over her head.

"Me, too." I hummed along to "You Are the Sunshine of My Life" as we walked to the coffee shop.

The air-conditioning made up for the duct tape on the seats and bad coffee. I ordered a club sandwich and a salad, followed by a bowl of chili and a slice of lemon meringue pie. We sat in silence until the food came, too tired and too discouraged to move.

"I'm trying really hard to keep a positive attitude," JT said, once she'd made headway on her Reuben.

"If only we could split up," Vina said. "A second car would have made this more efficient. Cell phones that worked out here would help too."

Geri laughed. "Technology? You think we could benefit from some?"

JT had to laugh, though I could tell it was an effort. "We are going about this rather low-tech, aren't we?"

I licked the last of the chilled lemon goo off my fork. "If I knew Mike's last name I could find him in a jiffy from work. He very likely pays taxes of some sort—he has delusions of respectability." I shrugged off a funny prickle in my neck and thought about ordering a sundae.

Vina blinked at me. "We know Ned's last name is probably Sandusky."

"That's right." Why hadn't I tried to look him up? "Well, Ned has no respectable qualities at all. I doubt he's ever filed a ten-forty." I wondered if I should call Carol in the morning and risk asking her for some help. Wait, tomorrow was Saturday.

"I wanted to kill Ned, you know," JT said abruptly. "I wanted to reach through the dream and rip it out by the roots."

"I know what you mean." I hunched my shoulders.

"What's wrong? Shoulder ache?" JT looked ready to launch into massage mode.

"No, just a funny fee—"

I can't tell you what made me turn my head. It was as if a faerie grabbed my nose and said, "Maddy, look over there." I don't believe in faeries, but Rose does.

From across the room I could only see the back of her head and one arm. It was enough. It had to be Tamar. Every nerve in my body said it was. The thick black hair I remembered tumbling over her shoulders when she had leaned over Sirena, the long nose and aristocratic neck—it was her.

One by one, my companions followed my line of sight. Rose was nodding with more and more certainty. Then, when Tamar turned her head to say something to the waitress we all knew.

She was gathering up her things.

"JT, I need something out of the motor home," Rose said. "Geri, pay the bill."

It was time for action, and Rose was in charge. I didn't question that, and from the speed with which JT handed over the keys and Geri scooted to the register, they didn't either.

Tamar walked right by us. Her skin was stretched over her angular face as if a great tension was burning her up from within. I didn't try to make eye contact; I was afraid she would somehow know me.

She wandered in the direction of the motel. Her steps were not the quick, focused speed I had expected.

Vina muttered, "She's not under her own name."

Rose hurried back from the motor home. "Julia, come with me. The rest of you stay close, but don't watch. Talk. Act nonchalant."

I matched Rose's quick pace toward Tamar. Behind us, following not quite as quickly, I heard Geri complain loudly about the heat.

"Excuse me," Rose called. "Are you from around here?"

Ahead of us, Tamar hesitated, then turned. She saw a group of women, and I knew her don't-talk-to-strangers reflex was assuaged. I noticed that she hadn't even broken a sweat in the evening swelter, which seemed unfair.

Rose was waving a map she'd pulled out of her pocket. We were in the middle of the motel/coffee shop parking lot, and I didn't know what Rose had in mind.

"Do you know if there're better places to stay in Harvard or Newberry Springs?"

"I'm from out of town," Tamar said. "I really don't know." She shrugged at Rose and turned away.

Rose closed in. She jammed the handle end of a screwdriver into Tamar's ribs and firmly gripped her arm. "We need to talk to you," she said.

"You must be kidding." Tamar looked like she was going to laugh, but Rose pressed harder with the screwdriver. "You're going to kidnap me? Are you fucking nuts? I should call the cops."

"You can't," Rose said coolly. "If you do you'll have to explain why you're letting two men hold a woman captive, and why you let one of them stab her—and why you didn't report any of it when you got back to town."

Tamar went white.

"It's to your benefit to come with us," I said. "I think you see that now."

She did. I had expected defiance, but instead I saw a wild hope surge up in her eyes, abating what seemed to be habitual anger and determination. "I'd be more likely to see it if you stopped jabbing me with whatever that is and told me who you are."

Geri and the others completed a circle around Tamar.

"You're Tamar Reese," I said. "You're going to pay Mike for doing a story on his little research project."

"Aren't you Little Miss Informed? Part of me knew she had to be carrying a transmitter somehow, and you've proven it." She shook Rose's grasp off her arm. "I can tell that's not a gun."

Rose's smile was so cool she seemed like a different person. "We wouldn't want anyone to get hurt, now would we?"

A pickup truck drove slowly by us, and I felt the driver's curiosity—a guy who saw a group of women. His feelings were all too predictable.

"This is not the best place to discuss all this," Vina said.

Rose slipped the screwdriver back in her pocket. "I think you're hooked."

"I'm not a fish," Tamar said.

"You're a poor excuse for a woman," JT muttered.

Tamar's lip curled into a bitter sneer. "You think I like what they're doing to her? You don't have a gun, but they do. And I have no idea where she is. The cops would be of no help, believe me. This is just not their jurisdiction."

"It's somebody's jurisdiction," Vina said. She looked as if she would add something, then changed her mind.

"Let's go back to the motor home," I suggested. "We can speak our minds more plainly there."

"Lead on, MacDuff," Tamar said, with an air of humoring all of us.

Her look was even more scornful when she saw the motor home. "Some cavalry," she said.

"At least we're the cavalry and not Benedict Arnold," JT said. "I can do without attitude from you."

"Vice versa," Tamar snapped. She stepped up into the motor home after Geri pulled out the steps.

JT turned on the lights, and Tamar took a seat at the table. I slid in across from her, then Rose perched on the edge of the short bench seat. The others sat on the little couch. To say the air was thick with tension was an understatement.

"You go first," Tamar said. "And then maybe I'll share. Start with how you know what you know."

"You're not in a position to make demands," Rose said flatly.

"If you want something from me you'll have to give me something first."

"You want something from us, too. This is mutual benefit here, not a one-way deal." I managed to maintain eye contact, but it was difficult. Her stare was daunting.

"Where is she?" Rose was having no trouble with eye contact.

"I wish I knew. If I did, I'd have her, not them. And I'd have all the cards."

"You're playing a game with a woman's life," Geri snapped. "How can you let this go on?"

"Because it's my life, too. And I'll tell you all about it, as soon as you tell me what you know."

:Maddy?:

:You're awake, I'm so glad. We found Tamar.:

:Can she help?:

:I don't know.:

:It's so hard to fight it. I'm so sleepy.:

:We're coming. Just stay in one piece!:

:I'll try. So hard...:

136

Sirena stiffened as Mike came in. He efficiently injected something into her IV.

:Nnnooooooooo..:

The drug hit her like a sledgehammer and then it reached for me. I dropped my head onto my arms. Tamar was telling the truth—she didn't know where Sirena was being held. Sirena was increasingly groggy and uncommunicative. I had this terrible feeling we were never going to find her.

"Julia?" Rose put her hand on my back.

"I need to lie down for a while," I said. "Just for a few minutes. He just put more stuff in her IV."

Tamar was gaping—I knew without looking. JT unrolled the foam pad, and I gratefully sank down onto it. Above me I heard them questioning Tamar and getting very little in return. Their voices were very far away.

I dreamed I was running, not from fear, but for the joy of it, across a cool, sandy expanse. I heard the concentrated breath of another runner on my left, and I veered to the right. She caught me anyway, and we tumbled over the soft sand. Her lips tasted of salt, and I relaxed in the shade of her platinum hair.

"That's everything," I ended. "All my mistakes, and wrong guesses, and why we're here." I wondered what had transpired while I slept. I had awakened to find Tamar sitting alone and everyone else trying to sleep. She had set up her little recorder and told me—truthfully—that I had been deputized to tell her what we knew.

Tamar was resting her chin on her hand. She hadn't spoken for hours and I had never in my life met anyone who could listen with such laser focus. "She's more heavily sedated than she was?"

I nodded. "Everything that happens to her happens to me. And since we're so much closer I can't fight it off. It would feel great to be sleeping again if I didn't know what it meant for her."

I don't know what Tamar saw as she stared out the window.

My night vision eyes could only discern cactus and rolling tumbleweeds. We were in the last possible spot of the campground. From here there was nothing but desert.

"So, have you decided we're nuts?"

"No," she answered. "I believe every word. And I hope you'll believe me—if you don't, JT will string me up."

"I'll know if you're telling the truth," I said.

"So you accept that you have psychic gifts?"

"No. I accept that she does and that I'm just her...conduit. That's the only explanation."

Tamar shrugged. "Well, let me tell you what I told them, which wasn't much. Okay? Then...I guess I'll tell you the rest."

I felt like a wrung-out rag. Rose stirred. I knew she had been awake all along. She hadn't interrupted so I suppose I had covered everything she thought was important. I sensed that JT had awakened a few minutes ago, but she too didn't seem to want to disturb us.

"First thing, I don't work for a real newspaper."

"We suspected as much."

"Are you going to comment on everything I say?" She widened her dark, brilliant eyes meaningfully.

"I'll listen." She had listened without comment to me for hours, so I could do the same.

"The rag I work for is the *National Weekly Star*, and its team of crack reporters consists of five people—one of whom is me—writing copy to fill a specified number of pages. I'm pages fourteen to twenty-eight, every week. If you think it sounds easy, think again. You can only do so many possessed toaster stories."

I opened my mouth to ask a question, but she quelled me with a glance.

"Yes, it's all made up. We read the other rags. Recently I've been wandering around in cyberspace keeping up with the latest kooks. I'm very good at telling fact from fiction. I've had to be. Not for the *Star*, but for myself."

Star. Could the Star from Jaja's reading be a tabloid paper filled with nothing but fiction? I reminded myself that I didn't believe in Jaja's nonsense but there was a distinct lack of conviction to my customary denial.

"We occasionally get called with information from crackpots, and our usual MO is to interview over the phone, change the names, add a bit of the window dressing, insert an official denial, and print it. What the *Star* doesn't do is send people out to investigate. I didn't tell Mike that when he called."

She hesitated, then glanced over her shoulder at JT. "You're up, right? Everybody's listening. Because I didn't tell you everything before."

"I'm up," JT said. Geri slithered out of the overcab bunk while Rose pulled herself into a more comfortable sitting position.

Vina went to the refrigerator. "If I don't have something cold I'll blow away." She handed around sodas from our replenished stock. Mine wasn't nearly as cold as I needed it to be.

"Like I said," Tamar continued after a long slug from her Diet Coke, "I can tell fact from fiction. I'm very good at that. And I knew Mike was telling the truth about what he had. And I had to see it for myself."

"She's not an *it*. She's flesh and blood, a human being. And she's in pain." JT shoved her hands under her thighs as if to keep from smacking Tamar.

Tamar blinked at her. "Well that answers my question. I wondered if you were just being coy—but you really don't know, do you?" Her emotions were a tangle of scorn and despair.

"Know what?" I was mystified by Tamar's sudden change of demeanor.

"Well. I'll get to that." She sighed and seemed lost in thought for a minute. Then she stirred. "We have to have an understanding. I believed you. You have to believe me."

"I told you," I reminded her. "I can tell if you're lying."

"And what about the rest of you?" She glanced down at Rose.

"Whatever Julia says is truth we'll believe," Vina said. "I've known her less than a week, but it's been an amazing week. She's pretty good at hiding from the truth, but she's never lied to me."

I was oddly touched by her belief in me. When Geri, JT and Rose nodded in support it kind of scared me.

"Okay," Tamar said. She addressed herself to me. "I didn't always work for that piece of garbage tabloid. Until three years ago I had a good job doing basic news coverage and police beat for the *Four Corners Morning Sun*. I could start the morning in Colorado writing up a piece about vandalism at Mesa Verde, then end the afternoon in Arizona with coverage of a helicopter rescue of rock climbers at Shiprock. It paid next to nothing, but my mother's mother was Navajo so that part of Arizona and New Mexico feels like home. At least it did, even though I wasn't raised on the reservation. My mother passed herself as white, and I grew up in Kansas City. She didn't want me to move near the res, but I like it. It's me." She looked out of the window again, studying the dark.

"Three years and a little bit ago I was leaving Gallup and heading home to Farmington. It was after midnight, but I'd driven the road a million times and very often been on it all by myself." She swallowed. "It's just a stretch of two-lane highway. Rises and falls, twists a little. Never saw any bright lights in the sky or flying saucers and pretty much thought anyone who said they had was a goofball. Even Hosteen Nakai, who was pretty sane about everything else."

She picked at the fraying edge of the window curtain. "And then it happened to me. One minute I was doing fifty, the next I was dead stopped and there was a bright light—bright doesn't even begin to explain it. You know how you can hold a flashlight up to your hand and it glows orange? I tried to shield my eyes with my arm, and the light came right through it." She shot me a suspicious glance. "I'm not making this up."

"I know," I said. She believed every word she was saying, but I was beginning to think she was delusional. This truth-telling skill of mine wasn't exactly foolproof. All I could tell was that she *thought* she was telling the truth about aliens. Give me a break.

140

"They took me...onto a ship, well I don't know about that. It could have been anywhere. What I know is that I was aware of their experiments. I knew they were taking my blood, reading my mind, examining every piece of my body." She blinked rapidly. "They were cold, and they didn't care that I knew what was going on. They didn't care when they hurt me, or humiliated me." She glanced at JT. "So while I'm sorry for what Mike is doing, a part of me thinks an eye for an eye, you know?"

My mind wasn't connecting the dots. "I don't follow you. What has any of this got to do with the woman Mike found in the desert?"

Tamar looked at me as if she'd never met anyone as stupid as I was. "She's one of them, don't you get it? The ones who took me. She doesn't look like them, but she has to be with them." Tamar's voice rose. "They put me back and I remembered everything they'd done. They took something I can never have again. I made the mistake of telling people. I lost my job, I lost everything I had because no one believed me. I thought I found a therapist who would help me, but he tried to get me admitted to a fucking psych ward." I felt the badly constructed seal on her anguish and rage come loose. "They took me apart bit and bit and didn't put it all back together the same way." She wiped away angry tears. "My boyfriend walked out because I couldn't bear him touching me. All I want is to find them and make them make me forget." Her voice broke. "I just want to forget it all. I thought you were with her, that she called you because you'd been taken, too. I thought you could help me but you can't. You can't even get across the fucking desert by yourselves."

For a few minutes there was only the sound of the wind and Tamar's choked sobs. Then JT offered her a box of tissues.

"Thanks," she muttered.

I didn't know what to think. I knew the others would turn to me for direction, but I don't believe in aliens or tarot readings or mind reading or any of the shit that had been happening to me. It was all so unfair. Why couldn't this have happened to Marigold

Jane Tempest, the New Age nut? She would have been in seventh heaven.

Finally, I found the courage to ask the question I didn't want answered. I knew what the answer was, and I didn't believe it. I couldn't believe it. "Tamar, are you trying to tell us that Sirena is an...alien? From outer space?"

Tamar sipped from the soda. "I'll take space aliens for two hundred, Alex. You really are a bit slow."

"You think you've been put through a wringer?" I couldn't keep an edge of hysteria out of my voice. "I don't believe a word of any of this. I don't believe it's really happening. I'm on the verge of deciding this is all a hallucination and I'm back in my bed under the influence of one of the little silver pills."

"Julia, think about it," Rose gently admonished me.

"I don't know what I believe, but I don't believe in little green men. *Star Trek* was just a show. I thought *Independence Day* was hokey, and the only thing that seemed real about the *Fifth Element* was the costumes. I only saw *Contact* because of Jodie Foster."

"Oh, she's not green." Tamar had a smug look I longed to wipe off her face. "Kind of coral-toffee colored, except her hair, which is almost pure white. And her blood looks like orange juice."

I shivered. I remembered Tamar saying "Holy Mother of God" after Mike stabbed Sirena's hand. My stomach was threatening to heave, just like when I'd seen the marks on Vina's wrist.

Tamar was studying me and nodding. "Now you're starting to understand. You're thinking why me? Why me? And there's no reason why. Your life will never be the same—" she smiled with false brightness "—for no reason at all."

Geri suddenly burst out laughing. Rose looked at her sharply. "It's okay," Geri said, through her giggles. "Julia, listen to the music."

David Bowie crooned, "Ground control to Major Tom." A hysterical laugh tried to break out of me, but I knew if I started I wouldn't stop.

Geri was trying to tell the others, but she could hardly speak.

Rose clambered over Vina and JT's legs to shake her gently. "Come on, Geri, don't let go. Hang on."

"It's Bowie's 'Space Oddity,'" I managed to choke out. "A little too real at the moment."

Geri gulped the stuffy, hot air of the motor home and calmed herself. "I'm sorry. It was too funny."

:*Maddy? Are you okay?*:

"She's awake," I announced. I felt the familiar swelling of welcome in me. I had missed her—I couldn't believe that this woman was some sort of alien manipulator. :*I'm okay. Just listening to some nonsense from Tamar.*:

Sirena didn't have to ask what Tamar had said, she just looked in my memory and knew. :*Maddy, I tried to tell you. I...was afraid you wouldn't help me. I've been so afraid. And then I liked you too much, and then you were so good to me, you helped me survive this, I just couldn't...*:

:*SHUT UP!*:

I was terrified, and then rage filled up the black hole created by the terror. :*You lied to me!*: I am such a fool. None of this was happening.

:*I withheld the whole truth. I never lied.*:

:*You've learned human semantics pretty well. You played me pretty well. You can't pronounce my name, Maddy, call me whatever you like. You don't know where I'm from, Maddy.*:

:*Well, you don't.*:

:*Slip in a little truth, and the big lie won't be so dishonest.*:

:*I am sorry. I can say nothing more than that. I wish I could have done this differently. I knew we would come to this.*:

:*Oh, are you adding omniscience to your list of skills? Telepathy's not enough for you?*:

:*We aren't that different, Maddy. I was studying your people because we are so similar. My people think that you are one of the Maker races, like us. We're scattered everywhere in this part of the galaxy.*:

I wanted to laugh. :*Yeah, we're just like you—Mike has proven that, hasn't he? Hold someone captive, play with their body and mind, like you did to Tamar?:*

She delved into my mind again, and all at once I hated the sensation. I'd come to enjoy it, even find it sexual, but no more. She'd played me for a fool just to get in my pants. "I have to get out of here for a bit," I said.

"Julia, what's she saying? Why is she so upset?" Vina had one hand on her heart.

"I don't care," I snapped. "I want her out of my head."

I practically fell down the steps on my way out into the night. I could see as if it were day and I was wearing sunglasses with gray/red lenses. *:You've altered me,:* I raged at her. *:Why should I help you?:*

:My people do not take specimens, not even nonsentient ones. We observe, we speculate, then we consider contact.:

:Tell me another one. Go ahead, I'm pretty fucking gullible. Help me, Maddy. I'm lonely, Maddy. Fuck me, Maddy.:

:I didn't ask you to do that!:

:No? Every time I let you, you picked apart my mind for my sexual memories, my fantasies. I let you do it, too. I wanted you to!: I pounded my fists on the picnic table. *:I can't believe I let you in.:*

:But you did—no one has ever given me such a gift. You helped me survive this long. I'd have gone mad without you. Maddy, I didn't mean to lie to you. I'm not perfect. I'm not...Vulcan. There is no such race, and if your people think there are, then they are in for a rude awakening.:

:I'm enjoying my awakening. This is such fun.: I wanted to call her names and push her out of my head. But I couldn't. Her apology didn't even begin to restore me to any sense of balance. I felt as if the world were slightly tipped and the only thing that kept me from toppling over was my link to her.

:Maddy, if you believe I am not from your world, is it so hard to believe there are other races out here with me? Tamar was taken by the Zzick—it has all signs of their handiwork. They won't stop, and my people haven't the power to make them stop.:

:I don't believe you.:

:If only I could show you. I showed you my world, my mother, my

sisters.:

:We were both asleep/awake, remember?:

:Maddy, I'm sorry.:

:I'll pay my therapy bill with your apologies.:

:I was not lying when I said I didn't know why you could hear me. I'm sorry I have hurt you.:

I stood on the very edge of the asphalt, watching the sand move and swirl around my feet. I nearly jumped out of my skin when I heard a step behind me.

It was Rose. "Are you going to be okay?"

I shook my head.

"I'm sorry, Julia. I suspected. I know someone with Tamar's story. I wondered. Then when Jake mentioned the meteor shower, the magnetic interference—"

"You decided an alien had been knocked out of the sky and into Mike's waiting arms."

Rose sighed. "From what Tamar says about Mike, he's been sitting in the desert for over twenty-five years waiting for this to happen. Monitoring radio frequencies, listening for space noise, wanting to be the one who makes first contact."

"Great. Another loony."

:Maddy, all I need is my hands free for ten seconds and I won't bother you anymore. Help me escape.:

I burst into tears. From the moment the first of my mother's boyfriends had molested me, my life had been in ruins. I'd rebuilt it, brick by stubborn brick, only to float in a meaningless job, endure a relationship where Marigold Jane Tempest had tried to make me into her version of a dyke, and now to end up in some third-rate sci-fi story without any special effects, no big budget stars. There was just me, four rather ordinary women, a dilapidated motor home, and a crazy reporter who told me the one person I'd ever felt safe with, ever opened my deepest wounds to, was from outer space. Great, my life was just hilariously great.

The wind sprinkled sand into my tears, and my eyes stung.

Rose was quiet, thankfully. She seemed to realize that comfort was not what I needed.

:I'll go away. You won't have to worry. You can put all this behind you.:

Of everything Sirena had ever said, of everything I'd learned about myself and this entire situation, the prospect of putting it all behind me was the most terrifying. As much as I hurt, as angry as I was at Sirena for her silence, at Tamar for telling me the truth, at Rose for being so damned calm about it, I knew one thing for sure: I did not want to put any of it behind me if that meant losing Sirena.

:Maddy, listen to me.:

:No.:

:I can't stay here.:

:I'm not listening to you.:

:People like Mike will hunt me down. Your government will hunt me down. I'll be a freak. I have to go, and there has to be no trace of me left.:

:I'm not listening to you.:

:It will only take a few seconds. I should have done it the moment I hit the ground, but I was so arrogant. I thought I could rest, find water, heal, then try to go home. I was a fool, and you're paying the price. I just need my hands free. And then you—you have to burn my body. I won't be in it anymore.:

:I'm not going to let you die.:

:I believe in the Wheel, Maddy. I don't die in fear. We have a ritual.:

:I don't give a damn. I won't lose you!:

"Julia?"

"Rose, we're having a fight, okay?"

I sensed Rose's smile and wanted to smack her. "Come back in when you're done."

:We'll find you, we'll get you out of there. I'm so mad at you, but I have to get to you. We'll set you free.:

:And then what? You have no means to return me to my home. I can't stay on your world. Our choices are very limited.:

:Look, we agree on one thing—we have to rescue you, okay? Promise me that when we do you won't go into your ritual thing right away. Give me...give me some time. Even if it's brief.:

She sighed because she knew I was telling myself I could change her mind. But she promised. Her promise gave me hope.

I looked up at the stars, remembering that last night I had known their names, known which ones were hot, which were cold, seen the planets rising. *:Thank you for the stars. I never noticed them before.:*

:Maddy, I would give you the stars and the moon if I could. My stars and my moon. But we have to be realistic.:

:You go right ahead. Reality has never been my strong point.:

I turned back to the motor home. We had a lot to do.

The sun was just rising.

Chapter 10

"What can I tell you?" Tamar's temper had worn thin an hour ago. She refused to believe that Sirena was not one of the race that had taken her. Cereal, Hostess Cupcakes and chocolate milk hadn't changed her mind. It had certainly made me feel lots better.

JT was still prickly with her, too, which didn't improve matters much. "Tell us everything, so we can help her."

"I've told you everything! They said Yermo was where I should stay. They picked me up and put a fucking blindfold on me, all right? Ned, that creep and a half, tried to feel me up when he helped me down out of that piece of garbage truck." Her lips twisted with something like triumph. "Even blindfolded I found his throat. I hope he's still eating soup. And before you ask—if any of you have the brains to think of it—there was no license plate on the truck."

"He took it out on Sirena." JT's anger was simple—she didn't care what or who Sirena was. She was being hurt and that meant she needed help.

Rose sipped her coffee. She'd already been to the showers, and her red hair was drying in tight waves. "Tamar, we're running out of time. Mike is sedating Sirena heavily. I think he's getting up his courage to do something—like an autopsy. I'm not sure he'll kill her first, either." She leaned forward, the cool demeanor that gave me the shivers in full evidence. "Now, maybe we haven't been clear about our goal. We're going to set her free. After that is up to her. You know something you haven't told us, I can feel it. We'll keep this up all day if we have to, and in the end you'll tell us what we want to know."

"Oh, I will, will I? Just how will you accomplish that?"

"I can be very persuasive," Rose said. There was a crack in her cool facade—it felt like sorrow and repentance to me. "Let's just say Mike is an amateur. I learned from people who are pros."

"Now, wait a minute," JT said quickly. "I'm not participating in this. No violence is ever good."

"It won't permanently harm you." Rose went on as if JT hadn't spoken. "But it'll hurt. A lot."

I was glad Geri was at the showers with Vina. Neither of them would have recognized this Rose. She scared me.

"I'm not kidding." JT leaned into Rose's line of vision. "Rose, I won't let you do this."

Tamar shifted on the bench seat. She glanced up at JT and then cracked a lopsided smile. "You're ruining her bluff." She looked back at Rose. "A very good bluff, too. But I know people, I can tell fact from fiction. Whatever you may have done in your past you'd give anything to forget it. You're not going to bring it all back over little ol' me."

"Don't bet on it."

"This is pointless," I interjected. "Tamar, if you could experience her mind the way we have you'd know she's not one of the ones who took you."

"That's just what she wants you to think."

"You said yourself she doesn't look anything like them. Don't let your desire for revenge cloud your judgment."

"Revenge?" Tamar shook her head as if to shake off memories. "Don't you listen? I don't want revenge. I just want to forget. I want to go back to New Mexico and not be crazy anymore."

:I can make her forget.: Sirena was somewhat fuzzy. The last dose of sedative had worn off, but she was still having trouble concentrating. She had figured out, however, that Mike only showed up when her heart rate went up, so remaining calm was the only hope she had of eventually clearing her thoughts.

"She says she can make you forget," I passed on. "I believe it too."

"If she's so powerful, then why don't I hear her?" Tamar showed her wrists. "No marks. No nightmares. No dreams at all."

:I sense her there with you because you perceive her feelings. When she was here she was not as blank to me as Mike and Ned. But she didn't answer my thoughts.:

I had a sudden thought. "You're straight, right?"

Tamar rolled her eyes. "Like ninety percent of the population."

"Maybe that's why you can't hear her even though you're now close to us, and you were close to her. Maybe because she's from a planet..." God, was I really talking about aliens and the planets they come from? I gulped. "A planet with only what she perceives as females—well, looks like female to us, maybe that's why she can talk to us."

"Wouldn't that be a convenient explanation? But you've hardly got a statistical sample to go on. And that hardly helps me think she can do anything for me."

:If I touch her with my fingertips I can make her forget. Zzick are blanks to us unless we touch them. I have no reason to think it will be any different with her. If I could touch Mike...if Ned had used my hand to...that night, then I would be out of here. My power is in my hands.:

"She says anyone she touches with her fingertips is usually readable to her."

"Oooo." Tamar was unimpressed. "Right out of *Babylon Five*."

Rose held up her hands. "What do you get out of not helping us?"

Tamar opened her mouth and shut it again.

"Right," Rose went on. "You get nothing. We offer you a chance at something. It's only a chance. And if you don't want it, then you can still help us and we'll leave you here."

Tamar sighed, and I felt her anger dissolve. "It's just that... I thought I had found one, you know? And I really don't know what else I can tell you."

"I've been making a list of things I want to know," Rose said. I thought she'd been doodling on her sketch pad. "For example, you said they have guns. What kind? How many?"

"I only saw one. Mike has it—I think he's smart enough to realize Ned can't be trusted with one. It's usually in the pocket of that phony lab coat he wears. I never saw bullets, by the way. Just the gun."

"What are the buildings like?"

"I only saw the inside of one. It was kind of a large barracks, like a military base. The room where she's kept is at one end. They set up a bed in the open area for me and locked me in at night. Whenever they took me over to eat I had to wear the blindfold. Paranoid jerks. I guess when I was talking to Mike is when Ned would—visit her."

"So you saw the inside of a dining hall," Rose commented.

"Yeah, I guess I did." Tamar looked at Rose with a glimmering of respect. "It wasn't a hall, just a kitchen. Mike's quarters, I think. It was too clean to be Ned's. We'd eat, and then they'd lead me back to the barracks. That's where Mike had all his reference stuff. Books and printouts and masses of paper. I mean this room was like eighty feet long, and there were tables and tables of papers and books and magazines. If they hadn't turned the lights off at night I would have studied it—not that it was organized. During the day Mike would rummage through stacks and haul out information he said I had to have to quote for my article. He had researched portable X-ray machines, knew where I could rent one, even, if I had a couple of thousand dollars."

"Are they expecting you to get in touch with them?" I

appreciated Rose's questions, but I wanted us to get moving. What Tamar was saying was all very interesting, but it didn't get us any closer to Sirena.

"No. After...after he stabbed her, I went back to pretending I thought it was all an elaborate fake. I was hoping he'd want to get rid of me so fast he'd forget the blindfold and I'd know my way back. But he just kept pulling out papers and books and telling me what I should put in my article. It's like he wasn't listening. Then all of a sudden he says I have to go—he doesn't want my money or my help."

JT grunted. "He found someone else."

"And that idea scares the shit out of me," I said. Though Tamar hadn't behaved in what I would call a moral fashion, I shuddered to think of what a truly unscrupulous person would encourage Mike to do.

"Have you any idea how long the drive took?"

"I looked at my watch before they put the blindfold on. Ned pushed me out into the parking lot about fifty-five minutes later. At least fifteen minutes of that was on good highway—we were probably doing between fifty and sixty. Before that we were on not-quite-so-good road for a few minutes, and before that it was unpaved road and we were creeping along." She broke off when Geri and Vina appeared at the door. "I decided to get a bite to eat, and then you all kidnapped me."

Vina looked cool and comfortable. She poured herself a cup of coffee. "That explains why you weren't registered at the motel."

"I didn't get a chance, thanks to you. Besides, I was going to sleep in my car. I don't have much in the bank, and since I haven't called in to work for four days now, I bet I'm unemployed. My life just keeps looking up."

Geri dropped a kiss on Rose's forehead. "You were right, the showers are utilitarian, but clean. And the water is refreshing." She glanced at Tamar and me. "You really should try it."

Wouldn't that be fun? All palsy-walsy in the shower with Tamar? Still, if we were going to get going anytime soon, I'd have to shower. I was too gritty and fragrant to imagine going without.

"You're not going to run out on us, are you?" Rose blocked the exit to Tamar.

"Holy Christ, woman, where did you get all this testosterone?" Tamar heaved a long-suffering sigh. "No, I'm not going to run out on you."

Rose flicked at glance at me. I nodded—Tamar was telling the truth. For what it was worth, she was going to stick around—for now.

Tamar went to get her gear while I headed to the shower. They were stark but clean, and the water seemed as rich as wine on my skin. I inhaled the mist deeply and felt Sirena drinking in the sensation of damp air. I became aware for the first time of her pain from cracked lips. How long had it been since water had passed her lips? Nearly three weeks?

:*Can you really not talk?*: While I resisted accepting any of Tamar's story as real, I knew it was a losing battle. I might as well learn as much about Sirena as I could.

:*I can vocalize, but not in your language. My speech would sound unintelligible to you.*:

:*Say something.*:

My head filled with mellifluous song. The closest comparison I could think of was whale song, but this was higher in pitch, sweeter and...I almost felt I could understand it. :*What did you say?*:

:*It's a poem.*: A gentle memory swept through her; I felt its lulling peace. :*A child's poem. It would translate to something like, 'Star look down, star hold me, star be my mother's arms, star lift me, star dream me, star so bright.' It's one of the first poems we teach our young ones.*:

Star light, star bright, I mused. All children look at the stars and wonder.

I rinsed shampoo out of my hair and with it what felt like a pound of dirt and sweat. I wanted to stay in the shower all day, but it wasn't going to happen.

I felt Tamar's presence as I was drying off. I struggled into my underwear and shorts while still partially damp, then slipped the only clean T-shirt I had left over my head. It was faded violet with still readable lettering: SACRAMENTO MARATHON 1995. As weak and spindly as I was feeling, it would be a long while before I ran another marathon.

I could sense Tamar's turmoil of emotions through the partition dividing us. They seemed so...loud. The anger she never quite let go of simmered, providing fuel for self-pity and confusion. I left the shower stall and brushed out my hair in front of the mirror. The sight of my red-ringed wrists no longer bothered me—Vina's were much worse. My reflection was all cheekbones and elbows. I wondered how much weight I'd lost. I was just about to leave when I heard Tamar swear softly.

"Are you okay?"

"Damn it all, my contact slipped. It's—ouch!"

"There's a good mirror out here."

"I'm not dressed," she snapped. "No free look-sees for the whole campground."

As if, I thought. There were less than a dozen vehicles in the campground, and I suspected most of those were just being stored. There was little chance anyone would come in. "There's no one here."

Her stall door opened, and I saw her clutching a threadbare towel across her chest with one hand while the other cupped her left eye. "Can you help?"

I stepped inside and closed the door. "I'm not very good at this. JT is the nurse."

"It's just slipped. Can you see it?"

I peered into her eye and saw the clear lens almost completely off the pupil, caught under her lower lid. "It's there. Down." She was trying to find it with her fingertip. "Left, that's the edge. You should feel it."

"I do. Oh man, that hurts. I'd rinse it out, but I lost my spare pair somewhere in that damn compound and I'm blind as a bat without them."

It looked good and stuck. Mari had occasionally had the same thing happen. "Do you want me to try to lift an edge? The more you press down, the more it's going to stick."

She nodded grimly, sitting down on the tiny bench. She tipped her head back.

The moment my fingertips touched her cheek and forehead I forgot about the contact lens. My mind was invaded with images of places and people I'd never known. Red rock structures, storm clouds over long mesas, a misshapen face with huge eyes looming over me, the sound of a dentist drill, screaming, the smell of my blood, the taste of it in my mouth. The drill withdrew and moved from my mouth to my shoulder and began again. The face never changed.

Tamar was frozen under me. Through a gray fog I saw that her eyes had rolled back. Was she breathing? Was I breathing? I saw her pain and humiliation, the complete degradation of her humanness, and I told her I understood. I told her she would survive. It was one of the things that women do best.

:Maddy, stop.:

There was more to her than what the Zzick had done. Once there had been laughter, a deep well of contentment. She looked out on the fantastical shapes of Monument Valley, and climbed the seven hundred stairs at Betatakin, breathed in the air as First Ones had. From the soft stone walls of Canyon de Chelley she watched the sunset in dazzling orange and pink, resting against the booted knee of a gentle-spirited man. The laughter of children playing in the river below was as timeless as the soft breeze, and she felt the stirring of the life within her—the sound of the drill—the smell of blood—and the child she would never know was purged from her body, and with it her wholeness and happiness.

He had wanted to believe her, but couldn't. Accused her of having an abortion and making up the flying saucer to cover it up. He just couldn't believe. I whispered to her mind that I believed her now.

:Maddy, you must stop. Now!:

I showed her what I knew of Sirena. I gave her the healing and love Sirena had given me. She shuddered and tried to push me away. Speaking to her mind, I told her I knew that when all you've embraced for years is anger and hate it was hard to hold anything else close to you. I showed her Sirena's compassion, showed her my own healing wounds—healing because Sirena had helped me believe that love could give.

Tamar's hands came to my waist. She pulled me down so I straddled her, and then she kissed me with an intensity that was so needful that it was beyond sexual. We breathed as one.

:Maddy, STOP!:

Sirena floated between our minds. She was sorting us out. Tamar...Maddy...there was a brilliant flash of platinum light, and then my fingertips were merely touching Tamar's face. Her lips were still hard on mine, then she gasped and turned her head.

I got off her lap and leaned against the door, feeling wobbly all over.

Tamar was blinking rapidly, then said in a cracking voice, "My contact is fine."

"I'll leave you alone then," I managed. I was too shaky to move far, but I fumbled with the door latch.

"Maddy."

How did she know that? I had found it hard in the past to meet her gaze, and this time was the hardest yet.

"Was that her?"

I nodded. "I didn't know that was going to happen." I had better be careful who I touched in the future.

"I know." She stood up, and the towel tumbled to the ground. One step, and she was close enough for me to smell the faint scent of shampoo. It made me dizzier.

She pulled my mouth down to hers. "I'm sorry," I felt her breathe into my mind. She wasn't talking to me. "I didn't know.

Thank you. I don't need to forget now—I want to remember you."

Sirena answered, but I was just the telephone line from her end. Tamar's kiss deepened. I'd been thinking about sex too much to ignore the heat of her body. That she was straight was not figuring very large in my response to her.

"Thank you," she whispered through me to Sirena. "My mother's people believe a debt should be paid with potent coin." Then, "But I can give you what I know you must be longing for. I feel it in both of you."

I was losing my sense of which way was up. Tamar pulled me into the shower area, still damp with steam. Her lips found mine again, urgent and tender. Her hands were under my shirt. "This is what she feels like," she told Sirena. "Her stomach, her hips, her back."

Tamar's hands were everywhere. I was fainting from desire and hunger, disoriented by Tamar's passion.

"Her neck is so soft." She lifted my shirt over my head, then her tongue traced my collarbone. "I didn't know a woman would feel like this...this is how her skin tastes."

:*Maddy, I can stop her.*: I felt Sirena's hard swallow, a match to my own.

:*No. I want you to know me.*: Know me, love me, stay with me. Tamar's mouth was on my breasts. I felt as if I would dissolve, that there was nothing to keep me in one piece. My atoms would release their hold on each other, and I would be able to dream myself a ladder to the stars...

I gripped the shower fixtures for dear life. Tamar knelt in front of me, pulling my shorts down. She lifted my foot onto the bench.

"Holy Mother of God," she breathed. "I didn't know it was so beautiful."

Sirena's cheeks were hot with tears. My body was like a rocket. I reached for her. :*Hold me, hold me.*:

Tamar looked as pale as I felt when she finally sat back on her

157

haunches. I gathered my clothes shakily, and after a few minutes Tamar began to dress as well.

When we were both clothed, Tamar spoke. "I'll help you every way I can. You have no idea what she did—"

"I do," I said. "She did it for me. The past is still there, but the pain is gone."

She swallowed nervously. It was a nice change for her to be evading eye contact. "I was just trying to help her. Give her something she longed for. Was it okay? I...I'd never thought of being with a woman before, though with my people it's not a crime. It didn't matter to me that you're not a man, I just wanted to give her something she needed. Did it help her?"

"Yes," I lied, with a soft smile that Tamar took for truth. Being a lesbian had given me Sirena, and for the first time I actually felt sorry for a woman who wasn't one. I also didn't want to explain to Tamar that she had helped me more than Sirena. Sirena now knew what she would be leaving behind, and from the ecstasy that had swelled from her to me through Tamar and back again, I was certain she would not be able to go. She would stay and somehow we would be okay.

By the time Tamar and I returned to the motor home, Mike had put more sedative in Sirena's IV. I could feel her fading out of my mind.

I should have felt like a pale imitation of myself, but I didn't. I was hungry, as usual, but even that was not an annoyance.

Rose and Geri were poring over the maps again. JT's first-aid kit was open on the floor, and she was applying gauze to Vina's wrists. Several blood-spotted swabs were clustered on a plastic bag.

Tamar was like a changed person. I saw Rose do a double take as Tamar leaned over Vina and gently asked, "Are you okay?"

Vina nodded, but she was pale. "Julia, what was happening a few minutes ago? I felt as if..." her color rose. "First I knew she was trying to get loose. My blisters opened. Then it was much more intimate. She was...blissful."

"My fault," Tamar said. "Maddy and I had a...disagreement, and then we found out that Sirena didn't need to touch me to... help. Maddy did it."

JT gave me a laser beam look when Tamar called me 'Maddy.'

Geri was puzzled. "What exactly happened?"

"I don't know," I said—which was partly true. I mean I know what Tamar did to me in the shower, but I didn't know quite what had happened when I'd first touched her face. "I don't think I want to experiment with anyone else. I touched her and I was...bombarded, I guess, with her memories. I don't think I was supposed to do that because Sirena got really upset. If she hadn't intervened we might have gotten..." I was at a loss for words.

"Stuck," Tamar said. "I remember her looking right at me and saying, 'You are Tamar,' and then Maddy was gone. There was just Sirena with me. And she"—Tamar blinked back tears—"I can't even describe it. More than healing, more than making me forget, she gave me peace. Like when you're a child and something hurts you and you run to your mother's arms." She wiped away a tear. "And you know you're safe, that nothing will hurt you again. When you grow older you learn that it isn't the truth, but the feeling of being held like that—I'd forgotten."

"So had I." I sniffled, then took a deep breath. "So today we find her and we give her back her life."

Rose looked very moved. "I'd love to know that feeling again myself."

I studied my fingers. "I don't think it'll work with her completely sedated. Mike visited again."

Rose cast an adoring look at Geri. "Oh, it's okay. I have Geri's arms."

"That's so sweet," Geri said.

Tamar laughed and her usual asperity returned. "Knock off the lovefest. You want me to lose my breakfast?"

JT finished with Vina's ankles, then packed up her kit.

She glanced up at me. "Speaking of which, you're probably starving."

I nodded vigorously. "I feel fine, but I could really use some food. Time's a-wasting, too."

Rose drew a circle on the map with her finger. "Well, given that they picked Yermo as the closest town with a motel, I'm guessing they're to the east of us. Fifteen miles east on I-15 puts us at this road. North is mountains and south is sand dunes."

"South," Tamar said. "I didn't have any impression of changing elevations. And the wind was completely unabated. When we were driving and in the barracks, I didn't have any sense of the wind coming around a building or a hill. It hit the entire side of the barracks all at once."

"Well, there's an installation of some sort right here." Rose had already marked it with a big X. "That's about five to seven miles south of the highway. We might be able to get there on an unimproved road not on the map. I made a line in my sketch, so some sort of road was on Jake's surveillance photos."

There was nothing but dry lakes out there, and in the distance something called Devil's Playground. That sounded friendly.

"Well, let's get some food, and then we'll head out," I said. "I want to stop at a store, too."

"I'd like to make a phone call," Vina said. "Just to check on things at home."

"And I need to check the oil of this old girl," JT said. "If I burn up the engine Esther will skin me alive."

:We're coming to you.: I knew she couldn't hear me, but my thoughts were almost singing. As we walked to the coffee shop I hummed along with "Dancing in the Moonlight." Perhaps tonight we would.

Chapter 11

I had learned something on this journey—every time it seemed like our objective was around the corner, we found a roadblock. I was so sure we'd find her right away that I should have expected we would not.

JT kicked the locked gate with all the ferocity I felt. My nerves had begun a slow thrum within a few miles of this turnoff—I knew we were closer to Sirena. I knew she was beyond that gate. Five-foot barbed wire fencing stretched for miles in both directions, but the dwelling itself was out of sight. There was no intercom or means to lure the occupants out or to trick them into letting us in.

"We're going to have to go back to Barstow for wire cutters. Dammit!" Rose kicked one of the motor home tires. "Such a simple thing. What kind of a terrorist have I turned into?"

Geri said hastily, "You're no kind of terrorist, thank God." She kicked a rock.

"This lock is penny-ante," Rose raged on. "Bolt cutters, wire cutters—anything more than a screwdriver and a tire iron, and we'd be through. I think they're counting on remoteness as their security. They'll probably see our dust long before we see them."

I looked up at the noon sun. It was dazzling and oppressively hot. I thought of the cool caress of the moon. "Then maybe we should go in after dark." None of us cast any kind of shadow, and I figured that if I believed Sirena was real, that she was from another planet, then I could believe some of Jaja's silliness. Follow the moon—it seemed like good advice.

"And how do we see where we're going?" JT stopped, then a slow smile spread over her face. "We don't have to—you can see just fine."

Rose seemed slightly mollified. "A pair of cheap wire cutters and we can go through fence instead of the gate...the road is level enough. We won't need lights. We'll probably see theirs and know when to stop. Then we can walk the rest of the way."

Geri wiped her forehead. "Can we please not stand in the sun? Let's talk and drive. And let's make sure we get everything we need, too, if we have to go all the way back to Barstow."

"No hardware stores in Yermo," Tamar said. "I wish I knew what kind of fencing the compound had. The barracks walls were cinder block."

"I couldn't tell from the surveillance photo." Rose clambered up the motor home steps. "I'd have made a note if I could have."

JT cranked the engine, and we trundled along the narrow road back to I-15. It would be well into the afternoon before we were outfitted, refueled, fed and ready for action. I had been tempted to go over the fence and walk in, but that was suicidal. I didn't even have sunblock, and the distilled water I'd bought was for Sirena. No, approaching the compound at night made more sense.

"Anybody who can grab a nap, should," I said. I received the incredulous glances I had expected.

Geri said it for everyone. "I had my three hours last night. Why would I need more?"

Tamar was the only one who didn't laugh. She sidled into the overcab bed, then looked down and stuck out her tongue at the lot of us. "I can take a nap. Neener, neener, neener."

Rose picked an ice cube out of her soda and threw it at Tamar. "Bitch," she said with a slight show of fondness.

"Ladies," Vina said. "Pax."

The thrum in my veins was fading as we drove west toward Barstow. Sirena was still at Mike's extremely untender mercy, and we were all joking like schoolgirls at a slumber party. And yet we seemed so close to our goal that a little high spirits wasn't unreasonable. Tonight would be soon enough. I was as convinced of that as I was of anything. Of course I'd been convinced of a lot during this trip, and been mostly wrong.

:Maddy, are you closer?:

:I think we're knock-knock-knocking on heaven's door.: I watched Rose efficiently snip the barbed wire. We'd acquired wire cutters, thick gloves, more distilled water, additional first-aid supplies, and heavy boots for me—my sneakers were not the wisest thing to wear in the night desert where scorpions roamed.

We'd finally started thinking ahead of ourselves, and not reacting to our dreams and emotions. JT was waiting in the motor home while Geri idled quietly in a rented Jeep. Tamar remembered a rough ride. If it got too rough for the motor home then we'd want four-wheel drive. It was in the back of everyone's mind we might have to make a quick exit, and maybe not via the road.

The motor home just squeaked through the fence posts, and Geri followed close behind. I joined Tamar and JT in the motor home while Rose and Vina followed in the Jeep. Vina looked exhausted and pale—she felt Sirena's physical pain far more than I did. The Jeep's air-conditioning probably felt like a slice of heaven to her.

"Eat something," JT said, for about the hundredth time.

I knew she was right. I'd been startled when I looked at myself in the mirror last. My collarbone was deeply defined and my eyes so bloodshot I looked like I had pinkeye. I felt fine, but I didn't look it.

I dug around in the cupboard until I found a half finished bag of Chex Mix. It made me thirsty, but drinking anything would be a challenge—the road was really lousy. JT couldn't go over ten miles per hour.

:You are getting closer.:

:I know. Slowly.:

:Maddy, I know you think I'll change my mind. But I can't stay with you.:

:We'll see. I've always liked this song.: I recalled the words to "Diamond Girl" easily. "Hey, Tamar."

She looked back at me from the passenger seat. "What?"

"What's with the music on Mike's radio? What does it mean?"

"Mean? It's pop music. It doesn't mean anything."

With exaggerated patience I said, "Why is it all from 'seventy-three? What does the year mean?"

"I dunno. Mike hid himself out here in 'seventy-four. He's got a huge reel-to-reel and set himself up a shortwave. The tapes looked like he bought them from a radio station archive."

I blinked. "I've been listening to every hackneyed song from nineteen seventy-three because that's what he was able to buy? It doesn't mean anything?"

Tamar shrugged. Geri was going to be furious.

I felt Sirena laugh—it was a wonderful feeling, like a melody rippling across my skin.

:Maddy, do you remember when I recognized that beautiful Bach piece? How I laughed and said if I ever got home I'd have lots to explain?:

:Yes.:

:Bach doesn't mean anything. It's just beautiful music. And now apparently the music I'm listening to here doesn't mean anything. And this music is driving you and Geri to distraction. But on Pallas there is an entire institute devoted to deciphering the meaning of Bach because your people broadcast that musical message from one of your space probes.

Since we first heard the broadcast from the probe we thought that music was the key to your people—it was so close to our own communication. We thought it was...a Rosetta Stone. But it isn't. One of my sisters is working on it.: She laughed again. :*I wish I could tell her she's wasting her time. She would be so...miffed at me.*:

It took a while, but the lightbulb finally clicked on. :*Voyager Two—the recordings onboard. Oh!*:

:*That's why we added your world to our explorations. You had a language we might be able to understand.*:

:*I can see how she might not appreciate the irony.*: I certainly wasn't terribly amused to find out I was hearing "Rocky Mountain High" for no reason at all. :*Your people have the wrong impression of us. That's our most civilized.*:

:*These men—they are the worst of you. The truth is somewhere in between.*:

"Tamar—that sucks," was all I said aloud.

"So sue me," she tossed over her shoulder. She and JT went back to what seemed to be an absorbing conversation. With her anger and rage stripped away there was something endearing about Tamar. I knew everyone felt it. I certainly did, and I don't think what happened in the shower had anything to do with it. Okay, maybe some.

I was really getting quite unskilled in the lying-to-myself department. Any number of people would be pleased about it— Maddy, crazy Maddy, was growing up.

We hit a huge pothole, and one of the cupboards burst open, spilling paper plates and supplies on the table and floor. It was too bumpy for me to attempt to clean it up, but I did manage to scoop a juice box and a bag of M&Ms off the floor. The candies were so warm the insides were melted. Yum.

JT let the motor home coast to a stop. "This is ridiculous. Esther will kill me if I seriously injure her pride and joy, so maybe we should just switch to the Jeep."

I was glad to step out into the night air for once. The Santa Anas had faded during the day, and the wind lacked the bite it had had as recently as last night. The full moon was rising, and we cast long shadows across the sand.

JT took one look at Vina and began fussing with the bandages she'd applied earlier. "You know, maybe you should stay here. I don't think you going in is wise."

"I didn't want to be the one to suggest it," Vina said, with obvious relief. She licked her cracked lips nervously. "I'd—I want to be there, to meet her, to talk to her. But I'll be more hindrance than help, I'm afraid. Walking is not very easy."

I hadn't realized just how physically ill Vina had become over the last two days. Her shoulders were hunched and every movement was cautious, as if pain was expected at any moment. JT was tsking over a newly opened welt on her chest—a match to the irritated patch on Sirena's chest from the tape holding the heart monitor sensors against her skin. If Vina was anything to judge by, Sirena was going to be a mess.

Rose knelt next to Vina. "I've been thinking someone should stay here, anyway. In case...in case we don't come back."

I felt a chill down my spine. I hadn't considered that possibility. I really had no idea what we were getting into. Everything was too real for a movie, and we didn't have super-commando powers.

"If we don't come back," Rose went on, "call the authorities. Call the CIA, call the FBI, call anyone. Call your friend Gladys. Get them out here. I don't think she'll be much better off, but if nothing else, Mike won't have her."

Vina flushed. "I'll call someone," she promised.

:Maddy, I only need my hands free for a few moments. I'll be gone. That's all you need to do—free my hands.:

:We're going to do more.:

:I can't do more. Maddy—I'm dying. I don't have the strength to get home. My vision is going. It's hard to hold a thought in my head. I was dead from the moment that meteor hit my deflectors. I should have released myself then. I've inflicted all of you with pain and anguish because I didn't follow the procedures I swore I would.:

:I'm not listening to this.: I was as forceful as I could manage.:*

166

We're rescuing you. Okay, after all you've put us through you have to give us a little time.:

:Time—well, after the accident I went through severe time phasing. I'm out of sync now. Even if I had the strength, I couldn't find the home strand. You'd call it a needle in a haystack.:

I didn't understand any of that, but it didn't matter. *:I'll help you.:*

:I know you want to. I know you would if you could. I've faced the truth—you have to as well. In the end, if you can set me free, I have to... Suicide is such an ugly word, the way you mean it. I'll go on the Great Wheel. That is the nature of life. I don't want to give up this one yet, by the name of all I love, I don't want to leave you, but I must. You must let me.:

:I'm not listening to this.:

"Julia, are you coming or not?"

Vina lingered at the foot of the motor home steps. I started to get into the Jeep, but something made me go back to her.

I was surprised at how frail she seemed in my arms. "Thank you for believing in me." I kissed her quickly on the cheek.

"The others are waiting," she said. And I caught something— a flicker of guilt? Probably because she wasn't going with us. She waved as we drove away.

I became the Seeing-Eye dog for Geri, pointing out potholes. We made better time, and with every mile Sirena grew stronger in me.

The motor home had long faded from view when Tamar suddenly squawked, "Look!"

At the edge of the horizon a light flickered. "That's it," I said. "Finally."

"Do you think light travels farther than sound?" Geri braked slowly.

"Hard to say," Rose said. "The wind is behind us, carrying our noise toward them, but it's a white noise of its own."

"We should walk from here," I said, suddenly certain. No one disagreed.

Walking or running on sand has never been my choice of exercise, and being in lousy condition it was really no fun at all. I carried the lightest load—a twenty-foot coil of rope in case we needed to climb a wall—and I heard the others struggling as much as I was. At least the wind was at our backs. Rose said it was a good omen, but every step felt to me like Heartbreak Hill, the wall, the twenty-third mile of the worst marathon of my life.

The lights never seemed to get any closer. I was reliving Sirena's run toward the white mountains with every step. If I hadn't understood her agony before, I understood it now.

I plodded along in the lead, the others literally following in my footsteps, picking out footing that avoided small scrub plants and holes made by desert creatures I didn't want to think about. I didn't know what day it was. I wondered if I should have called in to work that morning—no, it was Sunday, in the wee hours of the morning. There was really no way I'd be ready to go back to work on Monday. I didn't really care.

What was left of Julia Madison tried to do a reality check. I ought to be home, asleep. I should wake up in a few more hours, eat some decent food, rest, exercise a little, and then go to sleep again. On Monday morning I should get dressed and go to work. I should have lunch with Carol and get on with my life.

My life. What did Julia Madison's life mean to me anymore? What did work and that empty house mean?

:*It's who you are.*:

:*I'm not that person anymore.*: Sirena butted in at all the wrong times. :*That person doesn't believe in you, and she wouldn't be out here trying to save you. And she wouldn't believe that everything is going to be okay just because she wants it to be with all her heart.*:

:*This is all my fault. I'm in your mind, Maddy, that's why you think you can't live without me.*:

:*Don't start giving me human psychobabble crap. I still don't believe in that stuff. I believe in you. And I love you.*:

:*Oh Maddy...*:

Mike came into Sirena's room. I expected him to add more

sedative to her IV, but instead he turned down the drape over her and switched on the overhead light. I could hardly make him out in the glare, but he looked more haggard—and crazed—than ever.

"No one believes me," he said. "Not without proof. They were supposed to come today, but they say they won't unless I have proof."

Hmm, sounded like whomever was supposed to replace Tamar as the bankroll had backed out. That was good news. Good lord, if they'd arrived while we were out getting wire cutters I hated to think what would have happened.

He began a thorough physical examination of Sirena. I remembered from the first day the sensation of being poked and prodded. This was worse—Mike was not being gentle. He pulled on the fingers of Sirena's good hand until her knuckles cracked. Sirena caught a whiff of his alcohol-laden breath and I gagged.

"An extra joint, but they seem put together like ours." He bent her wrist back almost to the snapping point. I felt Sirena break out into a sweat, and I pitied Vina, who must feel as if she was being worked over.

I increased my pace. "Something's happening," I said over my shoulder. "I don't think it's good." I had to repeat myself twice because the wind snatched the words away.

The flickering lights were finally getting closer. The glow came from over a wall—at least six feet high I was guessing. As we drew closer, Tamar caught my arm and we all stopped.

"I'm sure this is it. Cinder block—corrugated steel roofing. This is it."

We finally struggled into the moonshadow of the wall. Just under the roofline were the high windows Sirena could see.

Rose whispered, "Everyone wait here and I'll walk all the way around. It's not very big."

Tamar patted her chest and pointed at Rose, then Rose nodded. They disappeared into the night.

JT quietly set down her burden—a gallon of distilled water

169

and her first-aid kit. I sensed a core of resolve in her that was heartening. She was scared, but determined.

Geri looked petrified, and the waves of fear I sensed from her matched her looks. She was trying to stay calm. I realized she was the only one of us with any sense.

I should have been scared shitless, but I wasn't. I set the ropes down quietly and leaned against the wall. It was still warm from the day's heat, and the warmth was soothing to my aching back muscles.

:*Maddy, how close are you?*:

:*We're at the wall. Maybe right outside your wall. We can't tell.*:

:*Wait for it...I can't think and do this at the same time.*:

:*Do what?*:

Then I felt it—a coolness spread over my body. I gasped and felt the wall behind me—it was cooling off rapidly. :*Sirena, are you doing that?*:

:*If you feel it you are on the other side of the wall from me.*:

I pressed my hands to the cool sensation and closed my eyes. I could almost see her, but Mike kept getting in the way. He pulled the drape down farther and kneaded Sirena's sunken stomach. He muttered about organs and skin.

I was startled by the return of Rose and Tamar.

"Well," Rose said in a low voice. "The main entrance is the only doorway in the walls, and it's very thick and very locked."

"Sirena's right through here," I said. I put my hand on the wall. "She's right there." I felt an odd wave of nostalgia when "The Entertainer" replaced "Hocus Pocus." Who knew that the music would lead me here?

"We have to go over the wall, then. Tamar and I were talking about it, and ringing the doorbell is not going to work because there's no doorbell."

"Mike's drunk. No sign of Ned. You're right. We startle them and there's no telling what they'll do."

Geri had stepped back to study the wall. She was shaking like a leaf, but she wasn't deterred. "I'm by far the lightest. I bet Julia and JT could boost me onto your shoulders, Rose, and I could go over."

"No, honey, I won't let you do that."

"Wait," I said. "Something's happening."

Mike had stopped prodding Sirena's hipbone. He stepped out of her line of sight, and then in stereo—inside my head and with my ears—I heard him bellow for Ned.

Ned answered unintelligibly. We could all hear the slow shuffle of his steps toward the large barracks. A door slammed, and after a few moments Ned came into Sirena's view. The sight of him sickened me. He looked at her with contempt. He'd used her and she was nothing to him.

"I want to turn her over."

"Sure," Ned said. "Different view."

Mike peeled the heart monitor leads from Sirena's chest. The tape took some of her skin with it, and Sirena shuddered.

Ned unbuckled the restraining strap across her thighs, then struggled with the strap around her left wrist. I held my breath. She had said that she only needed a hand free to be able to defend herself.

:*Maddy, I'm too weak. I was too weak when they caught me, and I'm worse off now. I can't overwhelm them.*:

Ned had the buckle undone.

:*Can you distract them? Can you do anything so we can sneak up on them?*:

:*I need to save my strength for the last thing that I must do. I can't change that.*:

Her hand came free, but it lay there, limp. He went to work on the other wrist strap.

:*Sirena! Please—don't do this. Not while I'm on this side of the wall. Please! Let me see you once. Then I'll help you do it. We've come so far... we can't lose you now.*:

"What's wrong, Julia?" Rose put her hand on my shoulder.

"Mike's turning her over, and they're freeing her hands. She's going to kill herself. She says it only takes a few seconds." Tears

171

streamed down my face. :*Sirena, please.*:

:*Maddy, I shouldn't love you. But I do.*: She was silent for the longest minute of my life. :*Wait a moment and you'll have your diversion.*:

Ned freed her other hand, and as he and Mike slowly turned her over I sensed her gathering what strength she had. Her hands twisted for a just a moment, then she slumped in near unconsciousness as her body screamed in pain at being moved after such a lengthy confinement.

She couldn't see Mike or Ned anymore, but I could hear them.

"That's gross," Ned said.

"Bedsores. Can't be helped."

The rage I'd felt when Mike had taken his first skin sample came back. It surged through me like a bolt of lightning. Adrenaline snapped my spine upright.

"Smells funny," Ned said. "Like something burning."

"Burning? It's not—shit!"

There was a lot of commotion as both men rushed out of the room. I heard exclamations of alarm, and then Rose was yanking on my arm.

I wasn't the only one with an adrenaline rush. In amazement I watched Rose jump, then pull herself onto the top of the wall. The cinder blocks were wide enough for her to perch. We passed up our supplies, and she dropped them on the ground below. I sighed with relief when the water jug didn't break.

JT boosted Geri up, and with Rose's help Geri was over. JT offered me her laced fingers, and after three attempts, with Tamar pushing my butt upward, I made it high enough for Rose to snag me by one arm. I went over the wall and fell in a heap on the other side.

Geri was dragging our gear into deeper shadow then coming back for me. I was still trying to gather my wits when JT came over the wall, landing neatly on her feet, followed by an equally graceful Tamar. Rose jumped lightly down.

172

The clamor from inside the barracks was abating. I looked around the compound. There were two small huts and the huge barracks. The open space was covered by dilapidated camouflage netting, below which was an astonishing collection of satellite dishes, antennae, radarscopes and other devices I couldn't even begin to identify.

And that was it. My anger increased—this was what we had been so afraid of? These puny men and their toys?

Then all of the lights went out—the music stopped. Geri sagged against the wall momentarily, her relief as evident as mine.

"Damn," I heard Tamar mutter.

"No," Rose whispered. "This is good."

:*Sirena, did you do that?*:

:*Yes. I can keep it up for a while.*:

After a moment Mike came out of the barracks. He walked right by us, then cursed when he walked into one of the pieces of equipment. He kicked at it.

"What's the problem, boss?" Ned came to the doorway.

"I don't know—the fucking generator. Go make sure she's not going anywhere."

"She's not," Ned called. Nevertheless, he disappeared into the barracks. I wanted to laugh when he too ran into something and cursed.

Mike was busy at the far end of the compound. I heard a rustling as JT drew a syringe out of her first-aid kit. She said in a low voice I almost couldn't hear, "This will work in about thirty seconds if someone holds him down. He'll be out for hours."

Rose grinned. "JT, you are an amazing woman."

"Better than knives and guns," she replied.

I swallowed nervously. I had envisioned us confronting Mike and Ned and convincing them to give us Sirena with the sheer power of our wills. How naive was I? "Rose and Geri, go with JT. I can sneak up on Ned—he's no powerhouse. Tamar and I can get him down and hold him until JT can get there."

Rose gave me a hard look, then nodded. Mike was banging on something in frustration, making enough noise to cover their approach. They had moonlight to guide them, and I had a feeling that Rose could handle herself. At least I hoped so.

I tucked Tamar's fingertips into my waistband, and we approached the door to the barracks. As we entered Ned disappeared into Sirena's room.

With Tamar nearly tripping on my heels we slowly went down a long, narrow aisle. I could see perfectly well. To each side were folding and card tables laden with masses of paper and computer printouts. Some had collapsed under their loads. There was no sense of the obsessive neatness Jake had taken with his surveillance photos—this was a madman's lair.

I heard Ned say to Sirena, "You can't get away." He scrabbled in the dark for something, and a sudden beam of light made Sirena blink. Ned had a flashlight.

"I was thinking maybe I'd have some fun while we wait for the lights, but you're disgusting."

His hand was on her hip. He picked at something and I wanted to scream. "Gross."

I slipped Tamar's hand free and ran. She'd find her way.

Ned didn't even see me coming—the flashlight was pointed at Sirena, and he just didn't expect an underweight, pathetically weak but completely enraged woman to fly through the door and grab him by the arm. I swung him hard into the counter, and when he sprawled against it I kicked him between the legs with every ounce of strength I had.

He dropped like a stone and let out a caterwaul that should have satisfied me, but it didn't. I dropped on top of him. For the moment I had the upper hand. He was bigger than I was, but I had my knee on his privates. I didn't care that it obviously hurt. I'd never felt so bloodthirsty in my life.

I sensed alarm from JT and Rose, then a swell of exultation. JT was on her way with the syringe.

Tamar burst in.

"Help Sirena get free," I said, glancing over my shoulder.

Ned took advantage of my distraction and threw me to one side. I held on, bore down with my knee.

:*Something in his right hand!*:

Sirena's warning made me look down. The knife must have been in his pocket, and he had managed to get at it. I ground my knee into his groin but I heard the snick of the switchblade ejecting.

:*Bastard! Sirena can't you do something, make him pass out?*:

:*He's a blank to me. There's nothing there.*:

:*He's not a blank to me! I know his type.*:

My rage coiled around Sirena's telepathy and coursed through my hands. That I had known decent men in my life meant nothing. He was a man, just like too many others, who thought women were toys, that hurting them was their prerogative.

His hand flicked, and I felt the blade nick me. He was trying to make me let go. I couldn't help but look into his eyes, and I saw there what I had seen too many times in the past. If I let go he would rape me, and then he would kill me. He would do it to all of us. He would do it for the rest of his life, whenever he could. I knew my rage was about the past, but my vengeance was about the future this monster would cause for innocent women and girls.

Maybe Sirena couldn't touch him mentally, but I could. All I needed was her power. Blinding, focused rage made me strong. I let go of his wrists and seized his head. Nothing seemed real to me but his eyes.

:*How does it feel to be a victim?*:

His eyes widened, and in his moment of surprise I poured all my anguish, the pain of violation, the years wasted in recovery, and every moment of suffering Sirena had felt, through the burning heat of my hands and into his brain. When my first fury was spent I deliberately played for him the first time I'd been raped by my mother's boyfriend, and he was me. I let him experience all of it.

He was crying when I let go of him.

:Stop crying. That didn't hurt. You know you liked it.:

My rage melted away, and I was so shaky I couldn't stand up. I had enough presence of mind to take the knife, but he didn't resist.

My stomach turned over when I realized what I'd done. I probed at his mind, but there was hardly anything there.

Sirena was weaving a little, but she was standing with Tamar's support. *:Maddy, what have you done?:*

:What I had to. I stopped him for good.: I gagged on bile.

The lights came on just as JT burst in the door. "What—" Her professional eye took in the scene. For a moment she inclined toward Ned's nearly lifeless form, then she turned her back on him and went to Sirena. "How can I help you?"

Sirena shook her head. *:Take me outside. Let me see the sky again, breathe the free air.:*

I wanted to drink in the sight of her. She was taller even than Tamar—six feet, I guessed. Her deep blue eyes were like stars. But I saw at once that she was suffering. She hadn't lied to me. It was written all over JT's face. Malnourished, flesh literally rotting on her bones: she was dying.

"Let's get her to the water. At least she can have that."

:If I'd found water they would have never caught me. It's...like chocolate to me. How did you know I longed for the feel of it one last time?:

:I know everything.: I ignored the suggestion that it would be the last time.

Rose joined us as we left the little room. She stopped short at the sight of Sirena's sagging body, tinted deep coral in the moonlight, supported between JT and Tamar. She reflexively crossed herself, then let them pass. "Geri's looking for Mike's gun—it wasn't in his pocket."

Tamar inclined her head toward Ned, who hadn't moved. "I don't think we'll need it. Maddy took care of that piece of filth. For good I hope."

176

I hurried ahead for the water. She'd gotten sick on food Mike had given her, but I was pretty certain that distilled water would be safe, no minerals or additives, just water. Two atoms of hydrogen, one atom of oxygen—our entire universe was built on it.

When I turned around with the jug in my hand, Sirena was tipping her head back, basking in the moonlight as if it were the sun in Saint-Tropez. She was smiling.

:Star look down, star hold me, star be my mother's arms...:

Chapter 12

:No...Sirena, not yet!:

:Don't worry, Maddy. It's just a child's rhyme. But I can't wait long.:

:I have the water.:

When she cupped her hands I saw the third joint in her fingers that Mike had mentioned. It made her fingers longer and more elegant to my eye than my own. I poured the water into her hands.

She let it spill down her arms as she sipped. An incredible feeling of well-being and delight filled me. I wanted to cry for joy. I felt an echo in my mind—Vina? She was crying, I thought, then abruptly my sense of her was gone, like someone threw a switch.

:I have given her healing and severed the link.: Sirena was smiling, then she swayed. JT and Rose helped her to a bench.

"We should have brought you some clothes," JT said. "Let me try antiseptic on these sores, please."

:There is no need for clothing and aid. Maddy, please tell her she has done enough. You have all done enough.:

I relayed Sirena's message and added, "If we'd done enough

you wouldn't have to...have to..."

:I must.:

I turned away. This was the moment I had dreaded.

There was a startled exclamation, then Geri's voice floated down from above us. "Rose, we've got a problem."

"What?" Rose hurried to a platform on the west side of the compound.

Sirena was lost in her own world. She slowly poured out the water and drank, then drizzled it on her thighs and back. JT appeared from one of the huts with a cooking pot full of tap water.

"Save the pure stuff for drinking," she said. "Can I pour this over you—the sores will sting."

Sirena's uplifted hands, reaching for the pot, was JT's answer. JT tipped the contents over Sirena's head, and the result was like liquid music in my veins. I swear that Sirena was glowing.

JT was grinning helplessly as she ran back to the hut for more.

:This is heavenly. Maddy, I never thought I'd feel water again.:

:We have lots of water. You don't have to go!:

:I must—but I do it with a singing heart, with the music of the elements in my head. I thought I'd lost them forever.:

I didn't understand exactly, but I knew she was suffused with a kind of joy I'd never known. JT returned with more water, then I was distracted by an urgent call from Rose.

"We've got company," she called down tersely.

"What?" I found enough energy to climb the short ladder up to the platform where Geri, Rose and Tamar were looking west.

There were lights to the west. It had taken us days to find this place, and now someone else was coming? I caught a flash of reflection on something metal. The only metal I could think of in that direction was the motor home.

"Vina," I said. "I hope she's okay." *:Sirena, can you link to Vina again?:*

:I think so,: she answered somewhat dreamily. *:Yes, she's there.:*

:What can you tell? Anything?:

:She is feeling much better, just as I am. I'm glad. But she's distressed. Someone is with her that I can almost link to... Someone I saw through you.:

Gladys. It had to be. I put together Vina's sudden need to call home, her guilt when we left her behind and came up with her calling the one law enforcement officer she could trust. I remembered her telling Tamar that this had to be someone's jurisdiction.

"It may be okay," I said. "It might be her friend Gladys."

The lights began to bob—they were moving. And it wasn't just one vehicle heading toward us, but four or five.

"Oh hell," Rose said. "If it's Gladys, she brought some friends."

:Vina is...sorry. She didn't know Gladys would call others.:

:Can you link to Gladys?:

:Perhaps. As she grows closer. There are blank places in her. She is determined.:

:Try, and try to send her back to Vina.:

"We have to get out of here," Rose said. "We're breaking and entering—"

"They don't know that," Tamar said. "With Ned and Mike out of commission we could be honored guests."

"And how do we explain Ned?" Rose glanced at me, but there was no condemnation in it. "Mike smells like a brewery, so we can pass him off as drunk—but when he wakes up he's going to turn us in."

"Maybe I can do something about it," I said. "Not like—not what I did to Ned. But maybe I can make him forget all of this."

:Maddy, that is not ethical.:

:Fuck ethics. I want you to live! I weigh your survival against all the Mikes in the world.:

I clambered down the ladder and over to where Mike's prone form lay next to the generator. I had no idea how to do what I'd suggested, but I knelt anyway, then hesitantly touched his forehead.

Next thing I knew, Rose was shaking me, hard.

"Julia, come out of it—what do you think you're doing? Are you crazy? You can't just jump into someone's mind!"

"What the hell do you know about it?"

"I believe in leprechauns, remember? Some of them will suck your memories dry, but they do have to be careful or they'll get overwhelmed and be forced to grant your wishes." She broke off, then chortled. "After what we've been through I didn't think anything would sound insane again."

I shook my head and felt clear. "Well, Mike's Looney Tunes. He's so paranoid that I mostly just got that from him. He's absolutely certain that humans in space brought back contagion with them. He worked for NASA at one point. Then he got sick, flu, who knows? But it was after meeting an astronaut from Skylab Three, so he's convinced that aliens tried to infect him. He won't use any equipment or read any books on science or listen to any music"—I glanced at Geri—"that is later than 'seventy-three. He thinks everything after that is contaminated."

Rose was shaking her head. "That explains this junk." She gestured at the motley collection of satellite dishes. "It's all so old, and most of it doesn't even work. And there's no computer in sight."

"His method worked well enough," Tamar said. "He went looking for something that fell out of the sky and found Sirena."

"Why did he torture her?" Geri glanced over her shoulder at Sirena and JT.

"I didn't...I didn't get close to that part of him. What I got was a burst of information, what he thinks about all the time. His reasons—they're buried pretty deep, and I don't think I can get there."

:And it's unethical.:

:You might have warned me I'd get overloaded.:

:Would you have listened?:

I wouldn't have, and she knew it.

181

"We don't have much time," Rose said. "The cops will be here any minute. They're not wasting time on stealth."

:Then I must go.:

:No!:

"We'll tell them that Ned and Mike kidnapped me," Tamar said. I could almost see the wheels of her mind spinning. "And you saw them do it so you followed them."

"Gladys knows differently."

I could hear the rumble of the approaching vehicles. There was a sensation of cool energy, and I whipped around to stare at Sirena.

:Sirena, stop!:

:I can't.: She grew brighter, then music—both like and unlike Bach—rang in my ears. *:Come closer, all of you.:*

Rose gasped. "Is that what she sounds like?"

I nodded, unable to speak. The others approached her on steady feet, but I stumbled, my mind incoherently pleading with her not to do this, not to leave me when I'd finally discovered how much I wanted to live.

She cupped JT's face. *:You need almost nothing. Such strength, and such desire to heal others.:* She took JT's hands in her own.

After a moment JT gasped and pulled her hands away. She stared at them, then turned to me. She gently took one of my wrists in her hand. It was suffused with warmth and when she took her hands away there was no trace of the red swelling that had been there moments before.

:You shall have this ability all your days, and so shall children of your body, and so shall their children. The potential was already there. All I've given you is a little boost.:

JT looked stunned. "This is an incredible gift."

Sirena turned to Geri, who stepped back. *:Don't be afraid. I have only so much strength, and I want to give some of it to all of you before I go. Let me give you something.:*

"I don't need anything," Geri said. "I just want to get home in one piece. I want Rose in one piece."

:I understand. This, then.: Her fingertips flitted over Geri's forehead. *:Sleep at will.:*

Geri grinned. "Okay, that I can handle."

Sirena turned to Rose, who stepped willingly into Sirena's embrace. When Sirena let go, Rose glowed with the same sense of wholeness that Tamar had radiated after contact with Sirena. She took Geri's hand, saying softly, "I've never forgiven myself for what I did when I was younger. But she looked right into my heart, saw it all, and she forgave me. I think I'm ready to make amends to the people I really hurt." She squeezed Geri's fingers. "And I think I'll sleep well, too."

Sirena had turned to Tamar. *:I don't need to read you to know what you long for.:*

Tamar's eyes widened as Sirena placed one palm on her own abdomen and one on Tamar's. *:Life.:*

They staggered apart after a moment, and Tamar went to her knees. She waved JT away. "I'm all right. It's...I'm okay." Then she began to smile.

:Don't your people have a Prime Directive?:

Sirena's search of my mind for a definition was quick. I savored the sensation, wondering if it would be the last time.

:What a novel concept. Noninterference. If we don't interfere, how will we ever make contact? You are so like us, and not that far behind in technology. You'll learn within fifty years how to fold space, and then you'll be...knock, knock, knockin' on our door.:

The sound of braking vehicles sent chills down my spine. It was over. Sirena would leave now. And I'd be so empty. She'd healed the wounds of my past, but I still didn't have the strength to build a future. What was I going to do?

:Maddy...:

:No!:

:Neither one of us wants to say good-bye—:

:You've been listening to too much pop music.:

A loudspeaker tore open the night. "This is the San Bernardino County Sheriff's Department. To anyone in there, come out with your hands in plain view. We have a warrant to search the premises."

I was too distraught for tears. My chest ached intolerably—it was beyond bearing. I slumped to the ground.

:Maddy, I must do it now. Don't be angry with me. Please don't hate me.:

:I don't.:

:You must help me.:

:Don't ask that of me. I can't!:

:You promised if I waited that you would help.:

The main door to the compound resounded from a heavy blow. The others jumped.

Sirena knelt next to me. Her skin, rinsed with all the water JT could carry in that short time, shimmered with brown and orange lights. Her thighs gave way to a triangle of silver hair. The familiar desire welled up in me. I wanted her so—but more than her body. I wanted her mind to stay with me. I would be so lost without the sensation of her thoughts.

She put one hand on my cheek. *:You can help by receiving my last energy. I don't have much left, but it's the most potent.:*

I tuned out the steady hammering on the main door to the compound, but I knew we had only a few minutes. *:You keep saying we're like you, but humans can't use their energy like this.:*

:Some already can. You'll learn to. It's simple once you know how.:

And suddenly I knew how. Her eyelids drooped, hiding dark blue centers. What should have been the whites of her eyes were actually pale pink, just as mine had been when I had last looked in the mirror. *:I can't teach an entire planet how to do this.:*

:You don't have to.: She was getting weaker while I was getting stronger. *:The others know now, too. And all those that my mind brushed, they know. Gladys knows. I sense her now. As I spread myself on the stars I sense all the minds I have touched.:* A gurgling sound came from her throat. *:They all know now. All of them...they're like you. Lesbians. Maddy, hold me.:*

She fell against me. I had thought I was beyond tears, but

184

I wasn't. They fell on her hair, her face and I rested her in my arms.

:*There are worse ways to die.*: Her body shuddered. :*Maddy, you must believe that you are an exceptional being. You answered me when no one else could. Just you. You're not powerless. You're not too wounded to go on.*:

I'd never felt more powerless in my life. Our link, always driven by her energy, began to waver, and I reinforced it with my own. I knew how to do that now.

For the first time I was looking into her mind. I saw the beauty of its arrangement, the serenity of her conception of the universe. I saw the science, stamina and mysticism that had brought her here. I saw a green world with coral skies and red oceans, I heard music, saw in a flash her mother, her sisters. And I saw the cords she was unraveling that bound her spirit to the body in my arms.

:*If you had the energy, how would you get home?*:

:*I've lost the time thread. I'm out of phase. If I could find it I would... it's easy, really.*:

:*You would build a ladder to the stars.*: I saw it in her mind. It was easy. It just took energy, far more than she had.

The compound doors creaked and something snapped. It wouldn't be long before we were overrun.

Then I felt JT's hand on my shoulders, and sensed through her Rose's hand in hers, from Rose to Geri, Geri to Tamar and Tamar's other hand on my other shoulder. A circle of energy.

My night eyes were dazzled with the glow that suffused Sirena's body. When she had her own strength she must look like this. Her eyes opened in puzzlement.

:*Sirena, look for the thread, hurry.*:

:*I must go—Maddy, this won't work, I'll never find it.*:

:*I thought I'd never find you. I thought none of this was real. Please try.*:

:*I'm too far out of phase. The threads are so small—*:

The singing in my veins I'd heard earlier, when she'd reveled

185

in water on her skin, was nothing like the music that poured through her at that moment. It sang of home, of stars and hope.

:Only you could make me believe the impossible.: She was slipping away. Her body was heavier in my arms while the light inside her began to slowly rise. It hovered for a moment, inches above her head. *:I'm going home.:*

The compound door gave way and there was a rush of heavy feet toward us.

All in an instant I let go of her body and threw myself upward, plunging my hands, wrists together, into the platinum light. I found my own cords. The circle of energy dissolved as JT lunged to catch my toppling body, but there was enough energy—more than enough. I wrapped myself in Sirena's being.

:Maddy, do you know what you're doing? It's not too late to go back!:

I looked down from where we hovered. JT was trying to resuscitate me. She would fail. The group of uniformed officers had paused, taking in the tableau. At the rear of the group was Vina, but she wasn't looking at the others, she was looking up—right at the light Sirena and I shared. Her face was streaked with tears, but her smile was brilliant.

All of my companions were looking up, except JT. Rose touched her hand to her lips in a gesture of farewell while Geri huddled against her. Tamar had one hand on her abdomen and she mouthed "Thank you."

We rose higher. Of the group of roughly a dozen uniformed figures, three suddenly pulled off their hats. I recognized Gladys's upturned face, but the other two women were strangers. Nevertheless, their tear-filled eyes tracked our rise as accurately as did the eyes of my companions. JT had given up her attempts to revive me, and she, too, looked upward.

We dreamed the ladder together until the stars held us.

Sirena flicked her mind and we went home.

186

Fresno Woman Dies in Cult Ritual

DATELINE—BARSTOW (AP). Julia Madison, resident of Fresno, died of apparent heart failure during a cult ritual, according to a San Bernardino Sheriff's Department official report released today. Madison's death occurred during a ritual in which alcohol and drugs played a part. The official statement also detailed FBI autopsy results on the alleged alien body found at the remote desert location near Devil's Playground when authorities broke into the cult compound after being tipped off that human sacrifice might occur.

The medical examiners found extensive surgical alterations that gave an as-yet-unidentified woman code-named Jane Doe 32 a "nonhuman appearance." The official statement did not cover the possible motives for making such alterations, but Sheriff Roger Tolan speculated that it was part of an elaborate fraud to lure sensation seekers to the cult. Jane Doe 32 died as a result of untreated surgical complications. The cult members have been released pending further investigation, but cult founder Michael Ross remains held without bail. An accomplice, Edward Sandusky, is wanted in Fresno County for parole violation, but remains at the County Mental Health Facility.

Madison is survived by her mother, Jennifer Madison of Reno. Friends and coworkers expressed disbelief at Madison's cult affiliation. Theodore Fisher, head of the University of California at Los Angeles Psychology Department, stated that, "Women such as Madison, childless, middle-aged, and employed in meaningless office work, are easy prey to dynamic men who offer them a magic cure for their dissatisfaction with life. In this case, it was contact with a so-called alien.

"Events like this always cause a rash of hysterical claims," Fisher went on to say. "We always expect an increase in claims of paranormal experiences after a so-called alien sighting." The UCLA Web site for reporting paranormal experiences, which researchers use in a program measuring social mental health, was shut down for several days after thousands of messages were received from what Fisher calls wishful-thinking people. "A story about an alien visitor circulates on the Internet and it spreads like wildfire, and the stories get more and more absurd. Everything from miraculous healing powers to women bearing alien babies. Then the tabloids get started," he said, referring to the National Weekly Star's banner headline LESBIANS GIVEN MYSTERIOUS ALIEN POWERS. Fisher concluded by saying, "Everyone is living in the new millennium and hoping some miracle will happen to solve the world's problems. Strangely enough, alien contact seems to give people hope. It's only human."

IT'S ALL SMOKE AND MIRRORS: The First Chronicles of Shawn Donnelly by Therese Szymanski. Join Therese Szymanski as she takes a walk on the sillier side of the gritty crime scene detective novel and introduces readers to her newest alternate personality—Shawn Donnelly.
ISBN: 978-1-59493-117-8
$13.95

THE ROAD HOME by Frankie J. Jones. As Lynn finds herself in one adventure after another, she discovers that true wealth may have very little to do with money after all.
ISBN: 978-1-59493-110-9
$13.95

IN DEEP WATERS: CRUISING THE SEAS by Karin Kallmaker and Radclyffe. Book passage on a deliciously sensual Mediterranean cruise with tour guides Radclyffe and Karin Kallmaker.
ISBN: 978-1-59493-111-6
$15.95

ALL THAT GLITTERS by Peggy J. Herring. Life is good for retired army colonel Marcel Robicheaux. Marcel is unprepared for the turn her life will take. She soon finds herself in the pursuit of a lifetime—searching for her missing mother and lover.
ISBN: 978-1-59493-107-9 $13.95

OUT OF LOVE by KG MacGregor. For Carmen Delallo and Judith O'Shea, falling in love proves to be the easy part.
ISBN: 978-1-59493-105-5
$13.95

BORDERLINE by Terri Breneman. Assistant Prosecuting attorney Toni Barston returns in the sequel to *Anticipation*.
ISBN: 978-1-59493-99-7
$13.95